ALEX WAGNER

The

Maus Trap

Penny Küfer Investigates

1

Penny Küfer was having trouble keeping her car on the road. Narrow, sharp and steep, the bends wound up the mountain, and the road was slick with ice. One stormy gust after another swept over the car, jolting it again and again, threatening to throw it off the track.

Fortunately, Penny was driving a low-profile car that didn't give much traction to the storm. She loved her high-powered black kitten, as she called it in tender moments, but the Jaguar sports coupe was definitely unsuitable for a mountain trip in a frigging ice storm. It turned more and more into a plaything of the elements the further she climbed the unprotected flank of the mountain.

More than once in the last thirty minutes the thought of turning back had crossed her mind, but she had gritted her teeth and kept going. She was moving almost at a walking pace, which of course was painfully prolonging the journey.

You're almost there, she said to herself for the fifth time—until finally, finally, at the end of the last switchback, the turnoff to a dirt road hove into view. It was wide enough for the car, but full of potholes.

From bad to worse! The Jaguar bumped along the trail, and Penny prayed that she wouldn't end up stranded somewhere.

It was only a little after four in the afternoon, but it was already pitch dark outside.

Penny squinted. It wasn't snowing, but the storm was swirling the snow that covered the ground and trees so much that she might as well have been driving through the middle of a blizzard.

Damn it all, this was a wonderful start to her vacation! Her *relaxing* vacation, as she had firmly resolved. If the journey to the hotel already felt like a survival trip on the slopes of the Himalayas, it was hardly a fitting start.

Another squall tore at the coupe, nearly sending it into a skid. Penny clung to the steering wheel, slammed on the brakes—and only just managed to keep the Jaguar on the road.

Once again she glared through the windshield.

She could make out an old brick wall with a wrought-iron gate standing open just twenty meters in front of her.

Vintage-style lanterns flanked the gate on both sides, and on the right there was a sign attached to the wall. It was half encrusted with ice, but the words were essentially still recognizable:

Bergschlössl zum Wilden Kaiser.

Wilder Kaiser—wild Emperor—was the name of the mountain range. *Berg* simply meant mountain—as if that fact had to be emphasized after the dizzying ascent!—and a *Schlössl* was a small castle. Her hotel! She had made it. She had reached her destination.

She carefully stepped on the accelerator, and her black kitten crept along the last few meters at a walking pace.

The storm acknowledged this with another howl, almost as if its fight against Penny was something personal and it wasn't yet ready to admit defeat.

Directly behind the entrance gate, the dirt road turned into a parking lot, which lined the hotel on the valley side.

Only a few cars were parked there, Penny noted with satisfaction. It was the end of November; the winter season had barely begun. And since the weather forecast was nightmarish for the whole of the following week, few spontaneous vacationers had strayed into the Bergschlössl.

It was just fine with Penny. She had deliberately chosen a hotel unlikely to be the sort of busy place where party people hung out; instead she had looked for a secluded refuge for those seeking peace and quiet.

Penny loved her job as a private detective—or rather as a security consultant, as she called herself officially. In particular, solving murders was her great passion. But she also had to unwind and chill for a bit in between cases! For this reason she had prescribed a few days of strict relaxation for herself, firmly turning her back on human malice and bloody murder. From today—Saturday—until Tuesday she would indulge in sweet idleness.

Up here in the Tyrolean Alps, at fourteen hundred meters above sea level, she was unlikely to stumble into another murder case, as had happened to her several times on previous vacation trips. In a place like this the most abominable crime might be the poaching of a deer once in a while.

The Bergschlössl was a small hotel, owned and run by a married couple. It boasted twenty-eight beds, in only fourteen comfortably-furnished castle rooms. There would be no bussed-in tourists, no skiers, not even wellness fanatics. The hotel advertised tranquility, tranquility, and more tranquility, supplemented by forest walks, down-to-earth cuisine and a marvelous alpine panorama, wherever the eye might wander.

Penny had opted for one of the forest rooms on the back side of the building, because she didn't intend to stand at the window and stare at snow-covered peaks anyway.

Mountains were all well and good, but she planned to make herself comfortable in the hotel's library or its lounge and stick her nose between book covers. A reading marathon—interrupted briefly at the most to stretch her legs and fill her belly with the much-praised local cuisine. A smile flitted across her face. A truly ambitious vacation program!

She got her luggage out of the trunk of the Jaguar and hurried toward the house. The temperature up here must be minus 15 or even 20 degrees Centigrade. And the howling storm made you almost feel like you were visiting the Arctic Circle.

The hotel had once been the country residence of a nobleman who had loved hunting the wild chamois, but architecturally it didn't really fit in with the Tyrolean mountain aesthetic. With its numerous gables and filigree turrets, and the richly-structured architecture, it looked more like a British manor house. The roof was a bit warped, and the paintwork on the facade was getting on in years.

Penny took an immediate liking to the place. Even from the outside it exuded charm and character, qualities she appreciated, and not only in old buildings.

The way the storm was raging outside, a spot in front of the hotel fireplace was only the more inviting. She would make herself comfortable in a recliner, put her feet up, and devour a few good mystery novels. That much crime was definitely permissible.

2

Barely half an hour later, Penny was already launching right into the middle of her planned vacation enjoyment.

The check-in had taken only a few minutes. Paulina Bachmair, the owner and operator of the Bergschlössl, had greeted her personally and then accompanied Penny to her room.

It was a spacious suite with a high ceiling, furnished with period pieces and exquisite textiles, homey, cozy, tranquil—and yet not too old-fashioned. Just right. There was a view into the deep snowy forest that covered the mountainside. The trees had thick white caps of snow, and bent under the heavy load. It was a landscape like something out of a winter fairy tale.

Penny had already unpacked her tiny suitcase. This time she hadn't brought a gun or any other equipment a professional of her standing would normally carry.

Instead, she had taken her new e-reader out of its protective case, put the few sweaters and jeans she had brought along with her into the closet—then she'd hurried down the magnificent wooden staircase and entered the lounge, which was located right next to the reception area.

It was a comfortable space that seemed like a cross between a bar and a living room. There was a counter with glass shelves behind it, crowded by a generous selection of spirits. Penny also spotted a futuristically-styled coffee machine and a large glass display case full of tempting-looking desserts. Tarts, muffins, cakes—a sweet, beautiful dream.

Dark leather fauteuils and sofas were grouped around low glass tables, and the end wall of the room was dominated by a marble fireplace in which a merry fire was crackling. On the walls hung copperplate engravings, prints, watercolors, mountain scenes from long ago, and in between, some modern art.

An elderly lady sat on one of the fauteuils just below the windows, bent intently over a crossword puzzle. She glanced up briefly as Penny approached her and nodded in greeting. The next moment she was already scribbling in her puzzle book again.

Penny guessed her to be in her early seventies. She wore a deep blue, high-necked sweater and a double-stranded pearl necklace. Her hair was almost white, quite short, and her lips shone pink.

Actually, she should be knitting or crocheting, Penny thought. *Then it would be just picture-perfect,* like out of a cozy mystery novel. But doing crossword puzzles was almost as good.

She looked around. Maybe there was a hotel cat, ready to cuddle up to her ankles at any moment? That would be the icing on the cake in this mountain idyll. So far there was none to be seen, but it could still appear.

Penny had to grin. It wasn't that long ago that she had

passed thirty. At her age others were still rushing from party to party, frequenting nightclubs and dreaming of vacations on Ibiza or Mallorca. She, on the other hand, had apparently turned into an old spinster who considered crossword puzzles and reading by the fireplace to be sexy.

She made herself comfortable in the sitting area directly in front of the open fire and took her e-reader out of her handbag.

Paulina Bachmair, the hotel proprietress, came rushing into the room through a back door as soon as Penny seated herself. Apparently she was also in charge of the lounge. In a small place like this, even more so in the early season, the owner had to pitch in more than usual.

Paulina and her husband—Simon Bachmair—had just taken over the hotel. Penny knew that much from the Bergschlössl website. As she had been curious, she had also read through their short dual biography under the header 'About Us.'

The Bachmairs were former stressed-out city dwellers who had run an insurance brokerage all their lives. For Simon's fiftieth birthday, however, they had made a long-cherished dream come true: their own small country hotel, away from the city noise and stress. The Bergschlössl had fit this vision perfectly.

Hopefully everything will work out for you guys, Penny thought silently. Running a hotel these days was no easy task; competition from private rentals like Airbnb had been putting pressure on prices for years, and hotels had to constantly fight to keep the available rooms well occupied. Even—or especially—if they only had a few of them available. And work certainly never stopped.

Paulina was small, somewhat chubby, and had brown hair in which strands of gray had already taken over. She apparently liked to dress in a somewhat eccentric style. Penny had already noticed that in the photo of the Bachmairs on their website. Next to Simon, who wore a dark, conservative suit, Paulina had looked like a colorful bird of paradise. Now she was wearing silky, baggy pants with a herringbone pattern and a pink blouse with batwing sleeves. Not exactly your typical Tyrolean hotel hostess.

Penny ordered hot chocolate, then turned on her e-reader. She had already downloaded several books at home, because although there was a guest WLAN in the hotel she didn't want to rely on its quality. There was no cell phone reception at all in the Bergschlössl— the Bachmairs even advertised this on their website. *Providing a stress-free vacation beyond the usual distractions*, was their motto. Next to the reception desk, Penny had already discovered an old-fashioned telephone booth upon her arrival—but that was the full extent of the Bergschlössl's telecommunications offerings.

Penny looked at the range of titles in her e-library. Which book should she read first?

She deliberated back and forth for a moment, then decided on a classic by Anthony Berkeley. *The Poisoned*

Chocolates Case. The title sounded promising. Chocolates were almost as good as hot chocolate, in Penny's opinion; sweets were her Achilles heel. But if you only *read* about pralines, at least it was a calorie-free treat. Poisoned chocolates—what an insidious murder weapon!

Penny gazed into the crackling fire and indulged in a daydream. As much as she loved to read murder mysteries and detective stories, wouldn't it make sense to put her own adventures on paper someday? Perhaps at the end of her career, when she was an old lady who could no longer actively hunt down murderers?

She had never tried her hand at writing before, and didn't think she had much talent in that area. But her own cases in book form—that was an appealing thought.

She indulged for a little while in the game of finding book titles for the murder cases she had solved in her career so far.

Her very first case—that was easy: *Murder on the Occident Express*!

And the second? Hmm, that was more difficult.

Death of a Snoop, perhaps? Yes, that didn't sound too bad.

A cool draft, followed by clacking heels, snapped Penny out of her amusing little daydream and brought her back to the present.

A blonde had just entered the room, bringing with her a rush of cold air from the entrance hall. She stood there for a moment, perplexed, and her gaze met

Penny's. A nervous smile flitted across the woman's face.

Then, on heels that were a good twelve centimeters high, she stalked toward a sofa that stood halfway between the old lady, sitting by the window with her crossword puzzle, and Penny's own armchair in front of the fireplace.

The woman, who might have been in her early forties, apparently had neither brought reading material nor a puzzle book with her. And no knitting needles either. She looked around again, probably in search of a waitress—but this time Paulina Bachmair didn't show up. She was probably busy elsewhere in the house.

"Hello," Penny said as the woman's gaze met hers for the second time. "Just arrived, too?"

The blonde nodded. "Yeah, that's right. Thought I wasn't going to make it. The world is coming to an end out there, isn't it?"

The woman hesitated for a moment, then stood up and approached Penny. She pointed to the free armchair on the opposite side of the fireplace.

"Do you mind if I join you? I'm pretty chilly, I'm afraid."

"Sure thing," Penny replied. She held out her hand to the blonde. "Penny Küfer—just escaped the storm, too," she said with a smile.

"Lissy Donner," the woman introduced herself. Then she dropped into the armchair and stretched her legs in the direction of the fire.

Penny wondered; the woman didn't fit in one bit with

the atmosphere of the Bergschlössl. She was not the kind of vacationer one would expect to find in a secluded country hotel in the Alps. In fact, she didn't look like a vacationer at all. More like she was at work—in the oldest trade in the world.

She had perfectly straight, golden blonde hair that fell almost to her waist. Her eyes were large and heavily accentuated with makeup. Her mouth also seemed almost too big for her face, but it gave her a very seductive smile. It reminded Penny of Julia Roberts, the actress.

However, Lissy Donner was also dressed like Julia Roberts, in her greatest movie success—*Pretty Woman*. In short, the woman looked exactly like a prostitute.

Her tight skirt barely covered her buttocks. Her top clung just as daringly to her curves and left almost nothing to the imagination. In addition, Lissy wore fishnet stockings with seams, and her red patent leather pumps had heels reminiscent of daggers, infinitely long and pointed.

Stop looking at people so critically, Penny admonished herself. At the sight of Lissy, her brain had started rattling and had immediately come up with all kinds of stories, from the fairly mundane all the way to the downright dangerous.

You're here on vacation, she reminded herself. People are good for a little small talk, but that's all. You're not here to reveal their darkest secrets—if they have any at all. Penny admitted that she occasionally tended to assume the worst right away.

16

When Paulina Bachmair finally did show up, Lissy ordered a double whiskey on the rocks. Then she did make some small talk with Penny, which felt however kind of forced. Lissy pointed to the e-reader that Penny had set aside and inquired about a few key technical features of the device.

"I've been wanting to get one of those for a while, too," she said. "Are you happy with it? What are you reading right now?"

Penny answered patiently and bravely refrained from pestering the woman with her own questions, knowing that their chat would have inevitably degenerated into an interrogation on Penny's part to find out what Lissy's unusual appearance was all about.

Next, Lissy switched to compliments. "Your hair is just gorgeous, Penny," she said, "Is it a natural red? And those wonderful curls. I'm so envious..."

When Paulina served the whiskey order shortly afterwards, Lissy immediately grabbed the glass with both hands, as if she needed something to hold on to. In frantic gulps, she started sipping the golden-brown liquid. The ice cubes clinked.

A wonderful contrast to the crackling of the fire, Penny thought.

The firewood gave off both a resinous scent and a soothing warmth. Outside, the storm was rattling the shutters with unrelenting fervor. Apparently it had become even more violent.

Penny was determined not to let her pleasant vacation mood be spoiled by the restlessness that her new acquaintance was radiating. But she found it difficult to achieve.

Judging from her facial expression, Lissy was not the sort of whiskey lover who wanted to enjoy her drink. With each sip she squinted, and seemed to not be really fond of the taste. Penny had the impression rather that she was trying to build up her courage.

After emptying the glass with a series of hasty gulps, Lissy rummaged around in her handbag. She pulled out a compact, flipped it open and looked at herself with a critical expression in its mirrored lid.

Then she abruptly jumped up. "See you later! Nice meeting you," she called out to Penny. "I'll see you at dinner, then?"

Penny nodded—and Lissy stalked off.

3

Penny didn't have to wait until dinner before she encountered Lissy Donner again. Not fifteen minutes later, her new acquaintance returned to the lounge—unsteady on her feet and in tears. She staggered over to Penny while wiping her eyes incessantly with the back of her hand.

Penny had trouble recognizing her, and not just because her tears had ruined her makeup. Lissy seemed to have changed. Her hair was no longer waist-length and golden blonde, but fell now in bland brown strands over her shoulders.

Penny set aside her e-reader and rubbed her eyes. She was usually a good observer. The woman must have been wearing a blonde wig. Well, it had kind of matched her outfit. But where had Lissy spent the last quarter of an hour? And what had shaken her so?

Lissy let herself fall into the armchair in which she had previously been sitting. She dropped her head into the palms of her hands and let her tears run freely.

The elderly lady at the window uttered a sound of displeasure, then bent lower over her crossword puzzle.

Penny sat there for a moment, perplexed, then stood up, walked the few steps over to her new acquaintance, and crouched down beside her. Carefully, she put her hand on the woman's shoulder. "What's the matter,

Lissy?"

The woman jerked her head up. Her face showed utter distress. "Men are such pigs!" she cried. "How could he? I tried so hard!"

"He?" Penny asked cautiously.

So Lissy had been meeting with a man. Was she really what she looked like? A prostitute—who had arranged to meet a customer here in the middle of nowhere? If so, the rendezvous had probably not gone well.

Lissy blinked away her tears and looked around the room. Her eyes fixed on Paulina, who was standing behind the bar counter, a little overwhelmed by all the drama.

"Can I get a double whiskey, please?" Lissy called to her.

"Y-yes, of course." Paulina immediately set about preparing the drink. She picked a suitable glass from the shelf and started filling it with ice cubes.

Lissy lowered her shoulders. Then she turned around as if looking for something. "Oh crap, I left my purse upstairs. Max just threw me out before I knew what hit me. Would you have a tissue for me, maybe?"

Penny grabbed her own purse from the back of her fauteuil and found a packet of tissues. She pulled one out and handed it to Lissy.

The woman's tears had dried up by now, but her face still shone wetly. The runny makeup had disfigured it into a chaotic, colorful grimace.

"Max is my husband," Lissy finally said, looking uncertainly into Penny's eyes. "I wanted to surprise him, and that's why I followed him here to the hotel. Hence my look. We like role-playing, you know...."

It took Penny a moment to understand. "So, um, your outfit is just a disguise?" she asked cautiously. *Now don't put your foot in it, Penny!* "And you were wearing a wig earlier?"

"Oh yeah. Don't tell me it really fooled you? Did you think I was a flesh-and-blood hooker?"

Penny nodded, barely noticeably.

Lissy laughed out loud, but at the same time new tears welled up in her eyes. "Well, at least I convinced you!" she sniffled. "That means I probably convinced Max, too. But he didn't like it at all. He hated it! He called me a vulgar slut—with a kinky imagination—because I found this particular role-play appealing."

Again, Lissy pressed the handkerchief to her eyes. "Oh man, I totally blew it. What am I going to do now? Max literally exploded. He—"

She faltered and gave Penny an uncertain look.

Penny's professional instincts had awakened. This woman obviously needed her help. "Your husband," she began carefully, "did he turn violent?"

Lissy lowered her eyes. "Max is a good man," she mumbled.

Penny interpreted that as a *yes.*

Paulina wordlessly served the whiskey—then stood there stiffly and silently for a moment. She seemed to be debating with herself whether she should interfere, but then decided against it and silently disappeared.

The crossword puzzler at the window acknowledged

her flight with an ill-tempered grumble. Presumably she had wanted the hotelier to chastise this guest who was so blatantly disgracing herself. Surely the elderly lady attached importance to spending her vacation in a respectable house. Guests who dressed up as prostitutes and thus caused a marital crisis were probably not in keeping with her idea of fun.

Lissy seized the whiskey glass, clasped it with both hands, and began to drink in fast, greedy gulps, almost as if she were merely quenching her thirst with a glass of lemonade.

Not a good idea, Penny thought. Large measures of alcohol were rarely the solution to any problem.

After Lissy had emptied the glass, she pressed her palms on the armrests of the fauteuil to push herself up.

"I'm leaving," she said, "right now. Max can get lost! I'm not going to put up with this!"

She got to her feet, but was swaying dangerously on her high heels.

"Wait," Penny said quickly. She couldn't possibly let the woman get behind the wheel of a car in this state.

Lissy had had at least two double whiskeys that Penny knew of. Maybe more. And she was emotionally upset. Not good conditions for a car ride in general, and certainly not on roads that were barely passable. The storm, howling around the house like an unleashed fury, was impossible to ignore.

"Did you book your own room at the hotel, Lissy?" Penny inquired.

The woman nodded. "Yes, I wanted to stay for the weekend. I thought I could sweeten Max's nights ... and leave him to his papers during the day. That's why he's here at the hotel, you know? To work. He does that a lot—books himself a room somewhere undisturbed. No cell phone reception—that's why he chose the Bergschlössl. That way he can work in peace and won't be interrupted all the time. Max is a very successful lawyer, you know. He has an insane amount of work to do."

There was unmistakable pride in her voice—and great love for her husband, even though he didn't seem to treat her too well.

Penny pointed toward the windows, where ice flowers were growing. "You should definitely use your room, Lissy, at least tonight. It's arctic conditions outside," she said. "I almost ran off the road on the way up here. And it certainly hasn't gotten any better since then: blizzard, black ice, the works."

Lissy stared uncertainly out into the darkness. Her lips opened as if she wanted to say something, but then she seemed to change her mind.

Penny gently grabbed her by the arm. "What do you say I escort you to your room? We'll stop by your husband's place, pick up your purse ... When I'm with you, I'm sure he won't pick another fight. Then you can have a nice bath, order dinner to your room, and in the morning, when you've had a good night's sleep, everything will look completely different. Maybe by then your husband will realize that he overreacted. And if not, I'm sure you'll be better off in the morning. On the roads, I mean."

Penny gestured with her head toward the whiskey glass and tightened the corners of her mouth.

Lissy stood there for a moment, undecided. "Alright," she said then. "Thank you so much, you're very kind, Penny. I'm really sorry to bug you with my marital problems!"

She swallowed. "That means, actually, we don't have any marital problems! I love my husband. And he loves me, too—or so I think. We've always had a lot of fun with our role-playing, ever since we met. He's been my prince, my knight, a mob boss ... even a vampire once. And I've seduced him as an elf, a nurse, a nun, a geisha, and whatever else came to mind. In this way, our relationship has remained fresh. We kept getting to know each other and falling in love over and over again."

She paused for a moment, seeming to think about something. "I really thought he would like my sexy bimbo," she said. She shrugged her shoulders and smiled wistfully.

"Look on the bright side," Penny tried to comfort her. "Your husband doesn't fancy prostitutes, apparently."

Lissy laughed in a shrill voice. "You really are the best! I feel so much better already. Thank you so much for being so helpful."

"You're welcome. Shall we?"

Penny started moving, and Lissy followed her without objection.

Out of the corner of her eye, Penny thought she saw relief on the face of the hotel's hostess, who had returned behind the bar counter. The old lady by the window, on the other hand, didn't even bat an eye as they passed her. She was either completely engrossed in her puzzle or was treating them with contempt.

Whatever, Penny didn't care. She would now safely maneuver Lissy to her room—hopefully without any major drama when they stopped by the husband's suite—and then return to her reading. Anthony Berkeley's poisoned chocolates.

At that moment, the lights went out in the lounge.

4

Lissy came to an abrupt stop and let out a small scream. "What's happened?" She grabbed Penny's arm, clawing at it painfully.

"Don't panic! Probably just a power outage," Penny said quickly. "Not surprising given the weather conditions."

Lissy blinked and inhaled audibly. "Yes, of course. Sorry, I guess I'm just feeling a little ... tense." She smiled thinly and pushed one of her mousey brown strands of hair behind her ear.

"That's all right," Penny said. "Come on, let's keep going." She pulled out her smartphone and turned on the small built-in flashlight. "This should do it."

Paulina did the same behind the serving counter; she too armed herself with her cell phone, providing light. "I'm going to check now," she said, "I'll be right back."

But then she paused, and her gaze wandered over to the crossword puzzler. Apparently, the old lady didn't have a cell phone with her, because she was sitting motionless in the dark.

"I'll light a candle for you before I check the fuses, Ms. Herzbruch," Paulina said, starting to rummage around behind the counter. "Or would you prefer to go up to your room as well? Then perhaps you could join Ms. Küfer?"

"A candle will do," the old lady said gracefully. "Thank you."

Penny nodded to the hotelier, then continued on her way. She left the lounge together with Lissy, crossed the entrance hall, and climbed the wooden staircase that led to the guest rooms on the second floor.

At the top of the stairs, a young woman came towards them. She was very pale, had strawberry blonde hair and wore a romantic flowery dress that reached her ankles. It was actually rather a garment for the summer.

The door to a room stood open behind her. It was the first on the right in a sequence of identical doors that lined the hallway to the left and right. Penny's own room was a little further back.

The young woman looked confused. "What's the matter?" she asked.

"Everything's fine," Penny said, "just a power outage, I guess."

"And the bang? What was that?"

"What kind of bang?"

"Didn't you hear them? They were quite loud. At first I thought of gunshots, several in quick succession. I only know that from television, of course," she quickly added. "But that's exactly what they sounded like. Did you really not hear it?"

"We were down in the lounge," Penny explained.

The woman nodded uncertainly. "Oh, okay. I'm sure I was mistaken. I mean, in a hotel like this ... there certainly wouldn't be any shootings." She smiled nervously.

"Certainly not," Penny confirmed. Still, an uneasy feeling crept over her. Gunshots? And then several in a row? The resulting noise was actually quite unmistakable.

Hopefully, the young woman's imagination really had run away with her. When the lights suddenly went out on a stormy night, such things could happen.

Penny turned to Lissy, who had stopped behind her. "What's your husband's room number?" she asked.

"It's 104. Right here on the left."

It was only a few steps to the door. It was closed.

Penny saw that Lissy was hesitant, so she went ahead and knocked on the door.

When she received no answer, she tried again, this time more energetically. But again there was no reply.

She tried the door handle—and found that it was not locked.

She pushed the door open a crack. "Mr. Donner? My name is Penny Küfer; I'm here with your wife. May we come in?"

She was greeted only by silence.

Penny hesitated for a moment. Lissy had not wanted to talk about it in detail, but her husband was apparently inclined toward violence. If his anger had not yet dissipated, and a stranger such as Penny burst into the middle of the marital dispute, she had to expect an unfriendly reception.

She took a deep breath, braced herself for what was to come, then entered the room. Lissy Donner followed close behind her.

The two crossed the short hallway and entered the bedroom. There—in the light of Penny's cell phone lamp—a devastating sight presented itself to them.

On the carpeted floor, in front of the large bed that dominated the room, a man was lying on his back. He was wearing black jeans and socks, his upper body naked. His legs were drawn up and his right arm stretched out to the side. The carpet beneath him shone a wet, bright red.

Blood.

Someone screamed—so loudly that Penny winced. It was Lissy.

The woman pushed past Penny. "Max? Oh God—"

Penny was just able to stop her. "Don't touch him, please! We can't help him anymore. Stay back."

All the life in Max Donner's half-open eyes had been extinguished. Three clearly-visible bullet holes were gaping in his bare chest.

The young woman in the flowery dress had not misheard.

Lissy pushed against Penny's arm once more, but then she obeyed. Swaying, she came to a stop. Her mouth was open, as if frozen in a scream.

Penny was careful not to step in the pool of blood. She approached the man from the left. *You must not destroy any evidence.*

She was sure he was beyond help, but she had to check.

She crouched down next to the man's head, felt for a pulse on his neck, held a hand right in front of his mouth and nose.

No breath, no heartbeat.

Lissy Donner was crying, but at least she wasn't screaming anymore. Like a drunk, she staggered over to the desk, where a black ladies' handbag made of embossed leather was lying. Probably hers, the one she had left behind earlier. With erratic movements, she rummaged through the bag—and finally pulled out a cell phone. She tapped the screen a few times, then pressed the device to her ear. "Police," she breathed to Penny.

But the very next moment she cursed and lowered the phone. "There's no signal!"

She stared at the display. "No reception. Damn, this can't be happening!" She walked unsteadily to the window, which was open despite the freezing cold, and stuck the phone out. "No reception here either."

She tapped the display a few more times, then returned to the desk and dropped the cell ungently. She sank onto the padded chair that stood in front of the desk.

Her eyes, swimming in tears, flitted over her husband's dead body. "Oh Max," she sobbed—then buried her face in her hands.

The fact that there was no cell phone reception didn't surprise Penny. After all, the Bachmairs emphasized that very fact on their website.

She turned around; a commotion had arisen in the hallway behind her. Footsteps, voices, a squealing scream. Several people crowded into the anteroom—at their head was Paulina, the hostess, armed with a tiny flashlight.

With quick steps, Penny ran toward her to block her entry into the bedroom.

"I-it's going to be a while before we have power," Paulina stammered as she stared transfixed at Max Donner's body. "Simon i-is checking the fuses in the basement." She stood stock-still, speaking mechanically, like a robot. She was obviously suffering from shock, unable to comprehend what she was seeing on the floor of one of her tranquil little hotel rooms.

Penny touched her arm. "I'm a detective, Paulina," she whispered to her. "I'll take care of everything, okay? Please go downstairs and call the police—as soon as the power is back on."

Without electrical power, the landline phone wouldn't work either, Penny surmised, but she wasn't 100 percent sure. It was a technical gap in her education that she would have to fill when the opportunity arose. The Internet, on the other hand, was certainly down, so they could not send a call for help to the police via e-mail for the time being.

But now the first thing to do was to secure the crime scene. That had top priority.

She addressed Paulina again: "Please take the guests downstairs to the lounge as well," she said, "and the staff. I'll just have a quick look around here, then I'll lock up and join you." She squinted past the small crowd toward the room's door—and found that the key was inside the lock.

She took another step toward Paulina to get her to leave. The people behind her—the young woman in the flowery dress and another woman—also backed away. Dazed, they let Penny maneuver them out of the room. Paulina seemed grateful that someone was telling her what to do.

5

After getting the women to leave the room, Penny dug her package of tissues out of her purse. She pulled one out, unfolded it, and used it to carefully turn the key in the lock.

She then returned to the bedroom. Lissy Donner was still sitting where she had left her, on the upholstered chair in front of the desk. Her eyes were fixed on her husband's body, her lips quivering.

Penny would have liked to have sent the woman who had just become a widow away, too, but she needed Lissy's memory while it was still fresh. She was probably the last person to have seen Max Donner alive.

It would be quite a while before the police appeared up here on the mountain, and in the meantime Penny wanted to do everything in her power to shed light on the matter. This murder case.

The detective in her had taken over quite automatically. The book-loving vacationer had had her day. To her own shame, Penny had to admit to herself that she didn't regret the abrupt end to her leisure time.

Lissy Donner sniffled softly. The sight of her dead husband was getting to her, there was no mistaking that. Or was she just putting on a good show? Had Lissy not only seen her husband last—but murdered him herself?

Penny looked around the room. Apart from the corpse, everything looked tidy, just as one would imagine a neat hotel room to be.

No fight had taken place here. And whoever had killed Max Donner must have acted quickly.

Lissy had been in this room a mere fifteen minutes ago, and had found her husband still alive on that occasion. That was by no means enough time to clean up the kind of chaos that came with a brawl. The killer must have shot Max before he'd even thought of fighting back.

Not half a meter away from the body, a gun was lying on the floor; it was most likely the murder weapon. Penny recognized that it was a Glock—she would leave everything else to the police experts.

She assumed that there were no fingerprints on the gun and that it could not be traced back to its owner. Even inexperienced killers were that clever these days. And there were hardly any hurdles in the 21st century to obtaining a stolen gun from an illegal source on the black market, or any other weapon for that matter.

Penny turned to Lissy. "I need you to focus right now, please. Okay? If we're going to catch your husband's killer, every observation you've made is important. Please look around and tell me if anything in this room is different than it was earlier. Any little thing could be relevant."

Lissy nodded like a frightened child. She jumped up and started pacing the room. However, she always kept the greatest possible distance between herself and her husband's body.

She glanced here and there while Penny gave her light with her cell phone. Ultimately, though, she shook her head. "I can't spot anything distinctive," she said. "The room looks the same as earlier."

"Was the window open when you were here before?" asked Penny.

"No, I don't think so. That is, I'm pretty sure it was closed. It's freezing cold in here, after all. And that certainly wasn't the case earlier."

"Okay, good. Can you tell if anything is missing? Were there things lying around that are gone now?"

"No, I don't think so."

"Nothing has been added either, I assume? Something the killer deliberately—or unintentionally—left behind?"

Lissy just shook her head again.

And Penny herself didn't recognize anything that didn't seem to belong here. In general, the room was almost perfectly tidy; apart from Lissy's handbag and the golden-blond wig she had worn earlier in the lounge, there was a newspaper and a miniature opened packet of potato chips on the desk. Probably a snack from the minibar.

On one of the bedside tables Penny noticed a closed laptop; next to it lay an expensive Swiss wristwatch. A black sweater hung on the backrest of the armchair that stood to the left of the window. The seat of the chair was occupied by a black briefcase, the sort one would expect a lawyer to carry.

It was a very ordinary guest room, like in any random hotel. If you disregarded the corpse on the floor.

Penny glanced over again at the wig lying on the desk. The artificial hair looked rather disheveled. "Did your husband rip the wig off your head—earlier, when you showed up here in his room?" she asked Lissy.

The latter nodded. "Max thought it was hideous. *The epitome of sluttiness,* were his words."

She sniffled, but then quickly changed the subject by pointing to the wristwatch on the nightstand. "I really can't imagine that Max was robbed. If he had been, surely the watch wouldn't be there. And anyway, a burglar, here in this ... mountain solitude?"

"Sounds unlikely, I know," Penny agreed with her. "But we can't rule anything out for now. The perp could have fled through the window because he heard us in the hallway, even before he started looking around for potential loot."

But this version of events simply didn't fit. If Max Donner had gotten in the way of a burglar, the man would not have shot him down without a second thought. Tyrol was not your average crime hotspot, where gangs ruled and homicide was common. Quite the contrary.

Penny walked the few steps across the room and leaned out the window. She was careful not to touch the sill or the glass.

Ice-cold air hit her face and the storm tore angrily at her hair. She recognized a rain gutter anchored to the facade of the house not half a meter to the right of the window. A reasonably athletic person could probably have climbed down that way. The room wasn't located high up; only the ground floor was below it, after all.

Directly under the window, a flowerbed lined the house. It was almost completely covered by snow. Only a few lavender bushes and low evergreen shrubs protruded through the white covering. Traces of a fugitive could not be made out from up here.

The flowerbed was perhaps one meter wide. Directly adjacent was the parking lot, which ran along the entire length of the house and was about six or seven meters wide. It was lined with lanterns that also illuminated the short stretch of road leading up to the gate. They were tiny specks of light in the darkness.

Wait a minute—why were those lights burning? Was there a separate power supply in the parking lot that had not failed?

The answer to this question became apparent to Penny upon closer inspection: Next to each of the old-fashioned lantern heads, she recognized shiny square panels. The outdoor lighting was powered by environmentally friendly solar cells.

The parking lot and the road were certainly cleared of snow regularly, but the storm had already turned them back into a landscape of white dune-like drifts. Most of the cars wore thick snow caps, Penny's black Jaguar among them.

Behind the parking lot, a wooded hillside dropped off steeply. Penny had already seen that much when she'd arrived here. From up here, she could only glimpse the dark tops of the trees, barely distinguishable from the night sky. The snow kicked up by the storm ruined any further view.

How could a potential burglar have made his escape? There were no visible tracks in the parking lot that indicated the recent departure of a vehicle. And on foot, an escape in this weather would border on a suicide mission.

Penny pulled her head back inside. Even though she didn't want to alter the crime scene, she decided to close the window. She didn't want the storm to make a complete mess in the room. Pulling out the handkerchief again she carefully closed the outer window wings.

Then she wrapped her arms around her body to warm up a little. At the same time, she turned to the widow again. "What kind of lawyer was your husband, Lissy?"

"He's ... he specialized in both business and family law," came the reply. "He didn't deal with dangerous criminals, if that's what you mean."

Penny knew what Lissy was getting at. A criminal defense attorney could, under certain circumstances, incur the hatred of a violent offender in the course of his work, who might later seek revenge. Perhaps because he felt he had been poorly represented at his trial.

In business matters, however, one could also have to deal with fairly villainous people. Lissy probably underestimated that a little. A dissatisfied client could have followed Max Donner up here into the mountain solitude—and made short work of him. But that sounded more like Chicago in the 1930s than the idyllic world of the Tyrolean Alps.

No, this version of events seemed too far-fetched. And anyway, how could a possible burglar or sinister avenger have actually gotten into the house? Had he simply marched through the lobby and advanced unhindered to the second floor?

After all, that was possible. The reception was not constantly manned, owing to the size of the hotel. You had to press a bell to make your presence known.

"Do you need anything from your purse?" Penny addressed Lissy one last time. "I think we should leave it here on the desk until Forensics has registered everything."

"No problem," Lissy sniffed. "I don't need anything."

"Okay. Then we'll go downstairs, okay? We'll lock up here until the police arrive."

I wonder why it's taking so long to restore the electricity, Penny thought as they descended the stairs in the narrow beam of her cell phone.

6

Paulina proved to be well organized and reliable despite the shock she had suffered. When Penny and Lissy entered the lounge, the hotel owner had already gathered most of the guests there and lit candles on the tables. "Only one gentleman is still missing," she explained to Penny. "Mr. Knaust went out earlier and I believe he has not yet returned."

Penny glanced around the room. Only a handful of people were present. "Are these all the guests you have in the hotel at the moment?" she asked.

Paulina furrowed her brow and bit her lower lip.

Penny had probably hit a sore spot there. The Bergschlössl was not large, but even for the slow season, the few people she saw here represented a dismal occupancy rate. The Bachmairs had certainly imagined the experience of taking over a hotel business to be very different, and certainly way more lucrative. And now, to make things worse, a murder....

"Nine guests are staying with us at the moment," Paulina explained with dignity. "Including you, Ms. Küfer." She rattled off a list of names from the top of her head: "Mr. and Mrs. Donner, who booked separately. Then four ladies traveling alone: Ms. Freyer, Ms. Maus, Ms. Sievers, Ms. Herzbruch. You would be the fifth, Ms. Küfer. And two gentlemen, also traveling alone: Mr. Lehmann and Mr. Knaust. Mr. Knaust is not currently in the house, as I said. He was not in his room when I went around to ask the guests to come to the lounge as you instructed me."

"Okay, thank you. And how many of the staff are in the hotel right now?"

"None at the moment. I sent Hanke home just before you arrived. Hanke is our cook. She was supposed to be on duty tonight, but I gave her the night off so she could make it to the valley before the roads became impassable. I always cook myself when she's off duty, you know. With so few guests, it's no problem at all; my husband and I like to do everything ourselves. It's a great way to cut costs, too. We—"

She interrupted herself abruptly. "Oh, why am I chattering away like a nervous chicken! It doesn't matter at all! Forgive me, I don't know where my head is at the moment."

"Not at all," Penny replied. "It's perfectly normal for you to be upset. You really don't have to apologize."

She gave the hotel hostess a caring smile, then gently asked further, "Apart from the cook, is there no other member of staff in the house? What about the maids?"

Paulina nodded, only to shake her head the next moment. "Yes, that's right, the maids." Her voice quivered. "No, they're not here right now either. We have two, but they work mornings. And they live down in the valley, not with us at the hotel. We do have rooms for the staff, but on days like today everyone prefers to be in their own homes."

She looked gloomily toward the windows, which were still being shaken by the storm.

"All right," Penny said. "Thanks, that's it for now."

She started to ponder. A very limited circle of people—that was good. A handful of guests and, of course, the Bachmairs themselves. They couldn't be excluded either. Nevertheless, the number of suspects she must consider for the murder of Max Donner was manageable.

Unless the murderer was in fact long gone. One guest was missing—Martin Knaust, whom Paulina had not been able to find. If he didn't show up, he would have to be dealt with as a priority, because in that case he'd be the prime suspect.

Penny turned toward the people who had gathered at the bar counter. Dark shadows were flickering across their faces in the light of the candles Paulina had set up.

Most of the guests had an alcoholic drink in front of them—and you couldn't blame them for it. Penny was eyed cautiously from all sides, and Lissy was being treated in much the same way.

Penny addressed Paulina once again. "We still don't have power," she said, stating the obvious. "So you haven't been able to call the police yet, I take it?"

Paulina's face contorted into a pained expression. "No, unfortunately. Simon, my husband, is still in the basement. I don't know what's taking him so long, but he's much better with the technical stuff than I am. I went to the office briefly, but of course everything is dead there. The phone system, the computers...." She shrugged, a helpless gesture.

At that moment a man came through the door behind the bar. He was very slim and dressed as eccentrically as Paulina was.

Simon Bachmair—Penny recognized him immediately, even though he had worn a conservative suit in the photo that graced the Bergschlössl website. Now bell-bottomed trousers, reminiscent of the hippie era, flowed around his legs, and he had paired them with a shirt that sported a dark blue paisley pattern. His hair reached almost down to his shoulders.

Apart from an old-fashioned flashlight, he carried with him a tattered rag, with which he was trying to clean his hands. His fingertips were covered in dark stains.

Lubricating oil or something similar, Penny speculated. Or maybe just dirt.

"Oh, here's Simon," Paulina introduced her husband. Addressing him, she explained: "Ms. Küfer is a new guest with us; she just checked in this afternoon. But she is also a detective by profession and has offered to assist us in this terrible matter. For which I am extremely grateful, Ms. Küfer," she added with a sideways glance at Penny. "I wouldn't know what to do..."

Simon Bachmair looked confused. "What's going on?" he asked—and only then did his wife seem to realize that he couldn't have known anything about the murder. After all, he had been in the basement to see what was wrong with the power supply.

Paulina began a confused description of the discovery of the body until her voice cracked to a halt and she gasped. Penny then took over the tale.

Simon Bachmair listened quietly while, as if on autopilot, he made the dirty rag disappear into a drawer under the counter.

"A murder?" he repeated, his eyes wide, when Penny had finished. "Here in the hotel with us?"

"I can't believe it either," his wife agreed with him hastily.

Simon gave Penny a strange look, then lowered his voice to a whisper. "There's something you should know, Ms. Küfer. This power outage..."

He hesitated, running his hand through his hair, staring at his wife.

"What is it, Simon?" Paulina asked in alarm. "Is there a major problem with the power supply? Have the fuses blown?"

Penny could tell by looking at the man that something was bothering him. Or was he even frightened? She looked at him questioningly, but did not press for an answer.

"Damn it, we've been sabotaged!" he blurted out. "The power supply didn't just fail—it was deliberately cut off! And irreparably so!"

7

Paulina gave a startled yelp, a small, sharp sound escaping her. "B-but that means..."

She braced herself on the counter with one hand and tried to fan air into her face with the other.

Simon nodded grimly. "That means the killer probably wanted to play it safe. No power—no communication with the outside world. It's as simple as that."

He looked at Penny, just as if he expected her to save them by conjuring up a solution out of thin air.

Which, of course, she was not in a position to do. Instead, she looked around the room, examining with a critical eye the guests of the hotel who had gathered in the lounge. Was one of these people, who all seemed like harmless vacationers, a saboteur and a murderer? Or had the culprit long since fled—out into the darkness and the snow?

Simon Bachmair had become so loud in his excitement that his last words had probably been heard in the larger part of the room.

A young man from the group closest to them looked over curiously.

Penny estimated him to be in his early thirties. He wasn't really obese, but a bit flabby and with a pear-shaped figure. He had short legs and fairly wide buttocks. His face was roundish, his hair blond but already visibly thinning, especially unusual for such a young man.

When Penny returned his gaze, he broke away from the group and came toward her.

"Ludwig Lehmann," he introduced himself. "I couldn't help but overhear..."

He broke off, then pointed with his hand toward the exit. "I can drive to the valley if you want. I own an all-terrain vehicle with four-wheeled drive. There will be cell phone reception further down the mountain, won't there? I could call the police from there."

Concern and also something like fear were reflected on his sweaty face.

"You'd have to go almost all the way down to the village," Simon Bachmair interposed. "The entire mountainside is a dead zone as far as mobile communications are concerned. We're not an area much frequented by tourists. There are only two farms here on our side of the mountain, and they're almost down in the valley, too."

"Then I'll go straight to the nearest police station," Ludwig replied. "It might be better if I report the incident in person anyway. The murder, I mean," he corrected himself.

The man was an attentive observer. It did not escape his notice that Penny was looking at him critically and pondering to herself.

For all she knew—and it was still far too little—this Mr. Lehmann could have shot Max Donner, and now he wanted to make off under a clever pretext. Instead of calling the police, he could slip away at his leisure.

Ludwig screwed up his face. "You don't think I had anything to do with this, do you?" he asked angrily. "I didn't know the guy at all! And I am a respectable citizen. The Bachmairs have my passport details, my address, my credit card. I'm just trying to help."

Penny ran through the options in her head. She could drive down to the valley herself to alert the police, but in her Jaguar that wasn't such a good idea, considering the current weather conditions.

Apart from that, the killer could still be in the house. It would be better if she stayed here with the group before another crime took place, or the situation escalated in some other way.

If Ludwig Lehmann really were to abscond, a police manhunt would track him down again. The young man certainly didn't look like a professional criminal; more like someone who spent his life comfortably in front of the television with too much popcorn.

But that was a prejudice, of course, and Penny knew it. Even the most dangerous serial killers or mob bosses sometimes looked like schoolboys.

"Thank you for your offer," she said to him. "I think it would be really helpful if you could drive down to the valley and alert the police."

"There's a station house just in the next village," Paulina said. "Do you have sat-nav in your car? I'll write down the address for you."

Ludwig answered in the affirmative. He dug his car keys out of his pants pocket and started moving. "I'll just get my jacket," he said, "then I'll drive down right away."

Only a few minutes after he'd disappeared, another man entered the lounge. He looked like a yeti; he had broad shoulders, was thickly muffled, and was covered in snow.

The newcomer paused for a moment, probably surprised that the lounge was so well attended and that everyone seemed to be staring at him. The conversations had fallen silent for a moment.

But then he peeled himself out of his jacket and headed for the group of women who had gathered at the bar counter.

"Can I have tea with rum, dear hostess?" he called out to Paulina.

Simon beat his wife to the punch. "I'm sorry, there are no hot drinks at the moment. We're having a power outage," he said. He managed to sound as if he was in complete control of the situation. "Would you like a drink, perhaps? Whiskey? Cognac?"

Penny turned to Paulina in a whisper, "Is this the missing guest? Mr. Knaust?" She eyed the man out of the corner of her eye, trying not to stare too obviously.

"Yes, exactly," came the reply. "Martin Knaust, from Vienna. As far as I know he's a fitness trainer, or something like that."

He definitely looked like someone who did sports regularly. He was a good 1.90 meters tall and built like an athlete. Only his face didn't quite match. Apart from his pink cheeks, which could be blamed on the cold, his tiny nose, thin and strongly arched eyebrows and full lips gave him a rather feminine appearance. He was still very young, twenty-five at most, Penny estimated.

"What's the matter, Christiane?" he said, turning to the woman standing next to him—a very elegantly dressed lady in her late forties. "Are you not feeling well?"

The woman looked as if she'd seen a ghost. Penny had noticed it before. She was ashen-faced and clung to the counter, with her hands cramping so much that veins stood out beneath her skin. "There's been a murder," she whispered. "One of the guests. Max Donner."

Martin Knaust looked confused. He didn't seem to understand what the woman was trying to tell him.

Either you're damn good at pretending, Penny thought, or you're actually completely surprised—and therefore innocent.

She rummaged in her handbag for her notebook and a pen and took up a position opposite the group, on the other side of the bar counter. Her place was reserved for the hosts, of course, but neither Paulina nor Simon seemed to mind in this particular situation.

It's going to take quite a while for Major Crimes to get here, Penny thought. At least she could do some preliminary work, and go through the personal data of the guests. Had any of them known the dead man—apart from his wife? And where had each of them been at the time of the murder?

Perhaps she could establish their alibis now already, and narrow down the circle of suspects somewhat.

Speculating that she would be able to solve the case before the official investigators arrived was unrealistic—but nevertheless Penny secretly cherished this hope. In any case, she would leave no stone unturned. It was clearly a fateful sign that the crime had happened right under her nose. And that, of all things, during her vacation!

By now the room was dead silent, and the eyes of everyone present were focused on her expectantly. The flickering candles on the counter made the distraught faces look even more sinister.

Penny grabbed her pen and turned to a new page in the notebook.

"My name is Penny Küfer," she introduced herself officially once again. At the same time, her gaze rested on Martin Knaust, who'd been the last one to show up. "I work in security consulting, and I'd like to help the police as much as I can in this murder case. Until the officers arrive, I'll ask you a few questions—with your permission, of course."

She looked around the room. No one protested. People seemed rather paralyzed and all too willing to let someone else take charge in this terrible situation.

"First, I will make brief notes of where everyone was when Max Donner was murdered," Penny continued, "and turn my notes over to the police afterward. Now, your memory is still fresh as to things you may have heard or seen. Please recall the last hour in as much detail as you can, and tell me everything, even if it may seem insignificant. Sometimes a seemingly trivial little thing ends up being crucial when it comes to convicting a murderer."

"You're acting as if you've already hunted down murderers single-handedly," the young fitness trainer said. It didn't sound unfriendly, not even particularly critical; more as if he wanted to joke, to lighten up the tense mood a bit.

"Believe it or not, I have. Several times," Penny replied. She really didn't want to brag, but that was just the way it was.

The young man's mouth hung open.

8

Penny stifled a smile. "Why don't we start with you, Mr. Knaust? Where did you just come from?"

His features darkened. "I certainly don't owe you an account," he snapped.

"Of course not," Penny replied patiently. "But we need to work together, don't we? A murder has occurred in our midst."

It sounded a bit like the words of a televangelist, she noted critically, but it didn't miss its mark.

Martin Knaust glanced again at his neighbor, the elegant middle-aged lady, then deigned to answer, albeit not very satisfactorily. "I was outside, stretching my legs a bit," he said.

"In the middle of a snowstorm?"

"Pah! I don't care about that. There is no such thing as bad weather, only improper clothing. A man does well to harden himself." His jaw muscles tightened.

"And how long were you out, uh, hardening yourself today, Mr. Knaust?"

"I jogged on the short trail through the woods. Maybe forty or fifty minutes. And I didn't even know the guy, before you ask. The dead guy. Haven't spoken a single word to this Max Donner since we got here. And I haven't seen or heard anything either."

Penny drew a question mark in her notebook under

his name, which she had already written down. It was a thoughtless scribble, not useful information. But she would let Martin Knaust's statement stand for now.

Next, she turned to the elegant lady standing next to the fitness trainer—which caused him to move even closer to the woman. Almost as if he wanted to ... hmm, protect her? Strange.

The woman gave Penny an agonized smile and began rattling off her information without being asked. "Christiane Maus, forty-nine years old, living in Vienna. Writer. I also did not know the deceased."

"Oh, I knew it was you, Ms. Maus!" someone exclaimed. It was the elderly lady who had been doing crossword puzzles in the lounge earlier. "The famous playwright!"

She pressed close to Christiane Maus, grabbed her hand and squeezed it passionately. It wouldn't have taken much for her to pull the writer into a bear hug.

"I recognized you right away," she chattered on, "but of course I didn't want to bother you on your vacation. Otherwise I would have dared to address you long ago. The Grande Dame of modern crime drama! Oh, it's such an honor to meet you in person—even under such tragic circumstances. I have seen every one of your plays, several times! Surely, as a crime expert, you can lend your experience to our young, er, detective here?" She gave Penny a skeptical sideways glance.

The name *Christiane Maus* was not unknown to Penny either. For several years Austrian and German theaters had been staging plays by this author by the dozen—from big cities to smaller provincial towns. They were all murder mysteries, and so popular that they found their way into even the most sophisticated houses. Even those theaters that otherwise liked to limit themselves to difficult, or incomprehensible, postmodern drama put plays from the pen of Christiane Maus on their programs—thus always ensuring sold-out houses.

Penny had already seen three or four of these shows herself—and had been thrilled. Ms. Maus knew how to stage exciting detective mysteries in unusual settings, and always came up with the most fantastic murder methods.

She eyed the lady, who had lowered her gaze with a touch of modesty. Her gray hair was cut youthfully short. On closer inspection, it was silvery rather, with a hint of violet. Not a natural gray, but a hair color that had recently become very popular among models.

Christiane Maus had a rather dominant nose, and an interesting but not classically beautiful face. Her lips were discreetly made up, but on her eyelids she had applied an intense, shiny metallic eye shadow in dark purple, which went very well with her unusual hair color.

Penny had to admit to herself that although she knew and appreciated the woman's plays, she had had no idea what Christiane Maus actually looked like until today. Authors were generally quiet stars who were rarely seen in the spotlight.

The playwright smiled melancholically and gave an apologetic look to the crossword puzzler who had come out as such an ardent fan. "I'm definitely not a useful detective—in real life, that is," she declared emphatically.

Of course, writing crime plays and solving real murder cases wasn't the same thing—but Penny still felt like she had just gotten backing from an experienced colleague. "Where were you at the time of the murder, Ms. Maus?" she asked.

Penny glanced at her wristwatch. "Mr. Donner must have been murdered between 6:15 and 6:30 p.m., from what we know so far."

At the word *murdered,* Ms. Maus winced. When she started to answer Penny's question, her voice failed her and only a pitiful croak came from her lips.

The author furrowed her brow, visibly annoyed with herself, and cleared her throat. Then she tried again. "I was in my room," she said, "in the bathroom. I didn't hear or see anything."

"No gunshots?" Penny asked.

"Don't press her so hard," Martin Knaust intervened abruptly. "Can't you see how shaken she is? Don't you have any sensitivity?"

Christiane Maus gave the man an unfriendly look. She was visibly uncomfortable with his solicitude. "Ms. Küfer didn't press me," she contradicted him. "And anyway, I can take very good care of myself!" Her words sounded unusually sharp.

"I understand all too well that you are frightened, my dear Christiane," the young man replied. "A murder ... it is so terrible. But nothing will happen to you, don't worry. I will see to that!"

Was there a history between Ms. Maus and the young fitness instructor? Penny wondered. It almost looked like it. But that didn't matter now. Her case concerned the murder of Max Donner, whom neither of them had known—at least if their statements were to be believed.

Penny decided to change her strategy. She didn't have time to question each of the people present individually and one after the other if she wanted to make any progress before the police arrived. Personal data and the like could and would be taken care of by the detectives themselves.

Therefore, she lowered her pen, looked around and said, "I have two questions for each of you. First, who among you knew Max Donner? Well, I mean apart from getting to know him here at the hotel."

None of the people present reacted. Everyone looked at the other group members to see if anyone would speak up. But no one raised their hand or uttered a word.

"Okay," Penny said. Thoughts were racing around in her head. A murder among strangers? That was unusual. In almost every murder case, the perpetrator and victim knew each other; it was the norm, except for bloodshed within the bounds of organized crime. And the Bergschlössl zum Wilden Kaiser was truly the wrong place for that.

Another strange occurrence was the sabotage of the power supply. Even more so considering it had taken place almost simultaneously with the murder.

This homicide was new territory, not a routine case.

Take heart, Penny, you can do this.

"So nobody knew Max Donner," she repeated, lost in thought. "Then let's move on to my second question: who of you was able to observe something that could be connected in any way with his death?"

This time, the hands of two women tentatively went up. "Fabia Sievers," one of the two ladies introduced herself without being asked.

It was the pale young woman in the flowery dress whom Penny had met on the landing on the second floor—shortly before she had discovered Max Donner's body. She already knew that Fabia had heard the shots.

She therefore turned to the other woman. "And you are?" she asked with an encouraging smile.

"Tamara Freyer," came the hesitant reply.

The woman looked deeply disturbed. She was perhaps in her mid-thirties, wore rimless glasses and a raven-black pageboy cut. "I have the room right next to Mr. Donner's," she said with trepidation, "and I heard something."

Penny looked at her expectantly. "Tell me, please."

Tamara nodded, barely perceptibly. "Of course, I didn't know ... that it was gunshots," she said. "I just heard a loud bang. That is, actually, it was several loud bangs."

She laughed nervously. "Oh, God, that's so awful."

Penny nodded in understanding. "If you agree—and you, too, Ms. Sievers—I'd like to have a chat with both of you. Preferably...."

She fell abruptly silent, looked around, then turned to Paulina. "Is there a room where we can have a private conversation?"

Paulina seemed to think for a moment. She looked as if the shock had paralyzed her. Then she turned her head slowly, raised her hand in slow-motion, and pointed to a door at the far end of the lounge. "In the library, perhaps?"

"Very well, thank you," Penny said. "May I start with you, Ms.—"

That was as far as she got. At that moment, the door that led into the lobby opened—and Ludwig Lehmann rushed in. He had his scarf wrapped tightly around the lower half of his face and seemed to be literally enveloped in a cloud of snow.

Penny stopped short. The young man who had so willingly offered his help could not possibly be back already. The drive down into the valley and the subsequent return to the Bergschlössl would take a good hour in such bad weather conditions, even with a cross-country vehicle that was well suited to the winter roads.

When Ludwig had freed himself from the scarf, naked fear was reflected in his eyes. "W-we're locked in," he stammered. "The main gate has been blocked. The saboteur has struck again!"

9

Ludwig Lehmann threw his jacket on the coat rack next to the door, then hurried straight toward Penny. Arriving at the bar counter, he heaved his big frame onto one of the stools that were still vacant.

"The saboteur has imprisoned us!" he repeated, looking at Penny with wide, frightened eyes. "The exit gate has been locked and additionally secured with a chain. There's something stuck in the keyhole, maybe a broken key. In any case, we don't have the slightest chance of getting that door open again. Not without a cutting torch!"

He spoke to the hotelier: "We don't have a chance to leave the parking lot, do we, Mrs. Bachmair? The wall runs across the entire front, I just noticed that. And at the back of the house, there's only the forest path. But it's much too narrow for a car. There is no way for us to get to the valley!"

Paulina Bachmair didn't have an answer. She blinked several times and seemed to look straight through Ludwig. Her husband was standing right next to her and looked similarly paralyzed.

Still, Penny had no doubt that Ludwig was correct in his observation.

It was Christiane Maus who finally spoke up: "That must have been the murderer's act," she said in an uncertain voice, "but what is he trying to achieve? I don't understand."

"One possibility is that the killer fled," Penny said, "and wanted to buy time that way. He made sure no one could follow him. Or rather, that we couldn't report the murder to the authorities. Hence the double sabotage: the power cut, therefore disabling the telephone, and following that the blocked gate."

She tried to recall the entrance gate to which she had paid only superficial attention when she'd arrived at the hotel. She saw massive cast-iron bars in front of her inner eye. The gate itself was set into a stone wall that was as high as a man.

Surely you could climb over it if you were reasonably athletic, but what good would that do? It was impossible to make it down into the valley on foot in this weather. You couldn't even reach the next house, which according to Simon Bachmair was almost down in the valley.

The saboteur had done a good job.

Penny addressed Paulina with a loud voice to wake her up: "How long would it take to get from here to the valley if you walked?"

Paulina moistened her lips, which looked very chapped, with her tongue. Then she said in a hoarse voice, "In that storm? A good four hours, I bet."

She seemed to have great difficulty speaking at first, but then she picked up speed. "The road is cleared only once a day. By now, I'm sure it's completely blown in. You would have to trudge through deep snow. And it's minus 24 degrees outside. I checked the thermometer earlier. And with the storm..."

She paused and shook her head. "You would freeze to death before you'd covered the first few kilometers!"

Penny nodded, lost in thought. It was just as she had imagined. On foot it was hopeless.

"Do you have skis in the house, perhaps? Or a sled?" she asked.

Now it was Simon Bachmair who regained his speech. "Sorry, no," he said slowly. "We're not big on winter sports, and neither are our guests, in general. We have Nordic walking sticks and some yoga mats, which we are happy to provide to our sporting guests. But no winter sports equipment."

Ludwig Lehmann groaned. "And now what?" He turned to Penny.

A very good question indeed. She had no answer for him.

"We'll have to wait until tomorrow morning," Martin Knaust suggested.

He was still leaning at the bar next to Christiane Maus, and had been talking to her for the last few minutes. Penny hadn't overheard their conversation— she was too busy with the problem she was facing.

"By tomorrow morning the storm will have subsided," Martin continued. "Then one of us can make our way down into the valley."

"One of us?" objected Violetta Herzbruch. The elderly lady eyed Martin critically. "You seem to me to be best suited for it. You are young and strong."

Martin nodded. A prideful expression spread across his face. "And that's why I will stay here and protect the ladies. That's the most important thing in our current situation!"

He gave Christiane Maus a meaningful look. "Someone else can run the errand. Him, for example." He pointed to Ludwig Lehmann. "A little exercise will certainly do him good."

"Get lost!" Ludwig snapped at him.

Martin acknowledged the insult with a startled expression that emphasized his feminine features, but then he regained his composure. He wrinkled his nose in disgust, but otherwise did not dignify Ludwig with a response.

Tamara Freyer glanced at Penny, asking, "Do you think, then, that the murderer is still among us? Are we risking our lives if we stay here at the hotel through the night?" Martin Knaust's heroic offer to protect the ladies had apparently made little impression on her.

Penny could relate. There was nothing protective about the young fitness trainer; instead he seemed rather sinister.

Now he had turned to Christiane Maus again and was talking to her in an insistent whisper. Penny couldn't understand his words—and Ms. Maus didn't seem the least bit interested. She looked pointedly past him and pretended he didn't even exist.

"We have little choice but to stay here for the night," Penny told Tamara. "Where else would we go? You've heard what conditions are like outside."

And even here, within these thick old walls, it would slowly become uncomfortable. Without electricity, the central heating boiler wouldn't work. It had already become quite chilly in the lounge—if you weren't sitting right in front of the open fireplace.

Fortunately there were quite a few old fireplaces in the house, where they could keep warming fires going. Even Penny's room had one, although it was rather small and probably more for decorative purposes than for real heating.

Hopefully the Bachmairs had stored enough wood. Otherwise, all the little group had left was their winter jackets and the warm blankets in the guest rooms.

Penny stood up. "I want to take a look around outside," she said.

She had to inspect the sabotaged entrance gate—and look around under the window of Max Donner's room, as she had intended to do from the very beginning.

If the murderer had escaped through the window, he was long gone. Perhaps he had planned his escape with the help of a car that he'd parked outside the Bachmairs' property. No one could track him—he had made sure of that by sabotaging the gate.

"I'll go get my jacket, take a look around outside, and then return to you," Penny told the others. "In the meantime, I think it's best if you all stay here in the lounge."

That way the guests of the Bergschlössl would be safe for the time being. And they could keep warm while they gathered around the fireplace.

Simon Bachmair left his place behind the bar counter. "I'm coming with you," he said, with a determination Penny hadn't thought he'd possess. "You don't want to head out there alone, do you? Maybe he's still around."

He did not have to elaborate further on who he meant by the little word *he*. The murderer, the saboteur. A man—or woman—who should not be underestimated.

That much was clear to Penny. "Okay, thank you," she said to Simon.

But at the same time she wondered if she could trust him, this seemingly caring hotel proprietor. Was his offer to accompany her in truth not a gentlemanly gesture, but a deadly trap? Was this aging hippie in reality a ruthless murderer?

It was hard to imagine, but appearances could be deceiving. Penny knew it all too well. She had been in mortal danger herself more than once during her past murder investigations.

Was Simon Bachmair planning an accident for Penny, out in the cold and dark? The opportunity was certainly favorable—but she would not make it easy for him. She would be on her guard!

She ran upstairs to her room, grabbed her well lined and hooded winter jacket, and then struggled out into the storm with Simon.

Minus 24 degrees Centigrade. Paulina's temperature reading was haunting Penny's mind. Combined with the storm, it felt more like minus 40 degrees. Not that she had any experience with such extreme temperatures. She wasn't the steely outdoor type; she felt much more at home on a cozy sofa.

They had hardly left the hotel when Penny was already freezing miserably, as if she were walking around outside dressed in nothing but a T-shirt. Her jacket was no match for the ice storm. The cold went straight to her bones.

"Let's make this quick," she said to Simon—and braced herself against the blizzard. She deliberately let him go ahead, determined not to turn her back on him under any circumstances.

The parking lot was already over-blown with snow, as if it had never been cleared. The solar lamps gave a dull light that was lost in the swirling white.

Penny glanced up at the front of the house. The second window on the first floor had to belong to Max Donner's room.

She pointed upward and gave Simon a questioning look. That was more effective than trying to shout up against the storm.

He understood immediately—and nodded. Yes, it was the room of the murdered man.

Simon pushed himself as close as possible to the protection of the house facade without stepping into the snow-heaped flower bed, which resembled a white sand dune. From the look on his face, he already seemed to be sorely regretting his offer to accompany Penny on her field trip. Maybe he wasn't a nefarious killer after all.

Penny came to stand just below the window of Max Donner's room and looked around.

The gutter was intact, and no footprints were visible in the narrow flower bed that lined the house wall.

This, however, was no definitive proof of anything. The storm would have blown away any tracks long ago—if there had ever been any.

She should have expected that. Penny shook her head in annoyance.

"Let's take a look at the gate," she yelled to Simon.

The two turned, braced themselves against the storm howling in their ears, and hurried down the short stretch of road that led to the main gate.

It was barely twenty meters, but the path seemed to drag on forever. Every footstep was pure torture. For three steps forward, they were pushed back two again in the next moment. The storm resisted them with all its might—and it knew no trace of fatigue.

You need to work on your fitness, old girl, Penny said to herself grimly. She was already starting to sweat, while at the same time she was freezing all over.

She asked Simon to stop a few meters before they reached the gate. "Don't cover any tracks if possible," she called out to him, although that was of course a flimsy excuse. But she preferred to keep him at a sufficient distance while she took a closer look at the sabotaged lock.

Ludwig Lehmann had reported diligently. The gate had been secured, additionally fastened with a bicycle chain, and something was indeed stuck in the lock.

Penny couldn't see exactly what it was, although she shone the flashlight of her cell phone directly into it.

Probably the key that belonged to this gate—the saboteur had made sure that it had been broken off in the keyhole.

In any case, one thing was certain: they would not be getting this gate open. Not tonight. And they wouldn't make it a single kilometer on foot, let alone all the way to the valley.

Penny tried to think back. When she had stood at the window upstairs in Max Donner's room and looked out, the gate had not yet been closed. She could have sworn to that. At that time—and from the first floor—the visibility had been better than here in the parking lot, where the swirling snow almost enveloped her. From the window, her gaze had glided along the path and then lingered on the wide-open gate as she'd pondered the murderer's possible escape route.

So the window of opportunity for the killer to have blocked the gate was quite narrow.

Penny had a problem with the chronology of events. The sabotage of the power supply in the basement must have happened almost simultaneously with the murder of Max Donner—and shortly thereafter someone had blocked the exit gate, at a time when Paulina Bachmair had been gathering all the guests of the Bergschlössl in the lounge.

Or rather, all but one.

10

When Penny and Simon returned to the lounge, Paulina was about to serve their guests a simple dinner.

"Just a *Brettljause* tonight: ham, cheese, some cold sausages and pickles," she told Penny, who was peeling out of her snow-crusted jacket.

Penny shook out the jacket—and realized in the next moment that she would have been better off doing that outside in the vestibule. She had left a conspicuous accumulation of snow on the floor.

Fortunately Simon Bachmair did the same. He patted out his jacket with his hand without even glancing at the floor. His thoughts, too, seemed to be completely elsewhere.

Paulina did not comment on the improper behavior with a single word. For the moment, she was fully absorbed in her role as hotel hostess, taking care of the physical well-being of her guests.

Penny found that rather touching, given the fact that there was a murdered man upstairs on the first floor of the cozy little hotel.

She decided to put the jacket, half freed of snow as it was, back on right away. It was clearly too cold in the lounge to just sit around in a sweater.

She headed for a free armchair that was still as close as possible to the fireplace. Most of the seats around the fire had meanwhile been occupied by the other hotel guests.

Paulina served one of the *Brettljause* plates to Ludwig Lehmann, who immediately began to eat with some appetite. She then returned to Penny.

"We had, of course, planned a multi-course hot menu for tonight," she explained, "but I've just had to improvise. I quickly made something simple—and decided to move dinner here into the lounge. Over in the dining room, we don't have a fireplace. It's already freezing cold in there. I don't know if serving food right now is even a good idea, though," she added, glancing around. "I think most of us have lost our appetites!"

A few of the guests, who already had plates in front of them, were poking listlessly at their food. Others had not touched anything yet.

Paulina looked at Penny questioningly. "And how did it go outside? Were you able to...." She faltered. "I don't know ... find some evidence, maybe?"

Penny shook her head. "No useful clues," she grumbled, "although in a way that can be significant, too."

Paulina didn't seem to understand. She just looked confused.

"The absence of clues is also a clue, is what I'm saying," Penny explained. She was frustrated that she was still no closer to finding Max Donner's killer, but cautioned herself not to throw in the towel too soon, either. That wasn't her style.

"I'll check the fuse box in the basement again," Simon said, standing around indecisively and rubbing his hands to warm them up. "I'm not a technician, but I might be able to improvise. If we can get the power back on, at least for a short while, we can finally call the police."

"Yes, you do that, darling," Paulina said. And turning to Penny she added, "I'll bring you some food in a minute."

"Don't bother," Penny replied, "I'm not hungry. If it's all right with you, I'll use your library for some one-on-one chats."

She pointed with her thumb to the door Paulina herself had indicated earlier—before Ludwig Lehmann had returned so abruptly from his thwarted trip to the valley.

Penny wanted to question Tamara Freyer and Fabia Sievers, the two women who had overheard the fatal shots, more closely.

"Yes, of course, the library is at your disposal," Paulina said quickly. "Whatever you can do—we are very grateful for your support!"

Fortunately, there was also an open fireplace in the library. Penny decided to take care of getting a fire going herself. A few moments later, however, she saw that Ludwig Lehmann had followed her.

"Wait, I'll help you," the chubby young man said as he gently pushed her aside. "This is a man's job."

Penny did not protest, although under normal circumstances she would have pointed out that she was not a mere helpless woman. Instead, she took the opportunity to ask him a question that had been haunting the back of her mind: "When you were in the parking lot earlier, Mr. Lehmann—did you run into Mr. Knaust? He returned to the house shortly after you left."

He raised his eyebrows. "Uh," he said, "I haven't seen him. But that doesn't mean anything. After all, you were just outside yourself. How do you judge the visibility? Maybe three or four meters? Ten, maybe, once the storm lets up a little?"

Penny had to agree with him. The two men could have passed each other in the parking lot without even noticing. Ludwig hadn't been looking for Martin, after all. He had probably hurried straight to his car, only to find that there was nowhere to go once he'd reached the gate. If he had looked around for people in the parking lot, he might have noticed a returning guest more easily, except for the fact that Martin could have circled around the back of the house, if he had indeed come out of the woods.

"There you go," Ludwig said, the fire crackling merrily away. "I guess we won't freeze to death tonight!"

Penny thanked him and together they returned to the lounge. There she approached Tamara Freyer. "Could we talk for a minute? In the library? You said earlier that you heard the shots fired at Max Donner, and I'd like to know more specifics."

As the two sat facing each other in front of the fireplace, surrounded by well-stocked bookshelves, Penny got right to the point. First, she asked Tamara for her personal data and the reason for her stay at the

Bergschlössl.

The woman provided the info without hesitation. "I am thirty-four, originally from Berlin. But I've been living in Vienna for almost ten years now, because of my job. I am an actress, you know. And as for my stay here at the hotel..."

She shrugged. "Nothing special, I just needed a few days off."

Was there a tiny hint of uncertainty in her voice? Penny wondered. Besides, Tamara had averted her eyes at her last words, which could indicate that she was lying.

Could indicate—but Penny couldn't be sure. Unfortunately, the matter of body language wasn't quite as simple and obvious as some 'experts' in the field liked to claim.

Penny thanked Tamara for the information, then asked, "You're in the room next to Mr. Donner's, you said?"

"That's right."

"And apart from the gunshots, could you hear anything else? Or maybe see anything? Were you in the hallway, or maybe looking out the window?"

"I'd been to the door a short while before. The wife of the ... murder victim,"—she seemed to have great difficulty uttering the word—"she came to the wrong door, and knocked on mine. She was super nervous and must have made a mistake. She wanted to see her husband, she said, when I opened. Well, to start with she was totally startled and couldn't get a word out. I think the poor thing thought I was her husband's sweetheart. Then when I told her he was staying in the room next door, she seemed pretty darn relieved. She apologized five times. Then she went over to his place, and I went back to my bedroom."

She paused for a moment, then continued, "Right after that, the two of them started to raise their voices. They were having quite a fight. Or rather, he got upset, and she tried to defend herself. I guess her outfit was too sexy for him. He yelled that he didn't want to be married to a hooker. So prudish, don't you think? He was actually quite nice looking. I wouldn't have taken him for such a square."

"Please try to remember the exact sequence," Penny said. "How exactly did things play out? How long were they arguing—what's your guess?"

"Only a few minutes, then Lissy just ran away. I heard the door slam shut and she ran past my room, sobbing loudly. She was uttering some rather nasty imprecations against her husband. I could hear it all quite clearly, although the walls and doors here in the house are way more massive than in most modern hotels I've been in. I think it's terrible to have to listen in on every hiccup your neighbor makes—if you know what I mean. But I digress. Where was I?"

"You could hear Lissy running away in tears..."

"Yeah, right. So: she ran off, and he went on a short rampage in his room. It sounded like he was banging his fist on a tabletop or something like that. Maybe also against the wall. And he was shouting at the same time.

Such a bitch!—something like that. Then he seemed to calm down."

"And how much time passed after that—before you heard the gunshots?"

"As I said, I wasn't even sure they were gunshots. Now, of course, I know better."

11

Tamara pulled her shoulders up and seemed to ponder for a few seconds. "It was just a loud bang," she said then, "that seemed to come from Max Donner's room. Three times in quick succession. And it did sound like the kind of gunshots you hear on TV, or even in a theater. It just seemed very unlikely to me that someone should be shooting around here in the Bergschlössl, of all places. You know?"

She smiled tensely. "So I didn't make much of it, because the power had gone out just before. And I—"

"Just a minute," Penny interrupted. "The power went out *before* the shooting? Are you sure about that?"

Tamara nodded. "I think so, yes. Yes, definitely. Does it matter?"

"Quite possibly," Penny said, "but please, continue."

Tamara looked at her silently for a moment. Then she stared up at the ceiling, as if she had lost her train of thought and had to think about what she had just reported.

Finally she said, "So the lights went out. Then the three shots were fired. In quick succession—but I already said that, didn't I? To be honest, the thought crossed my mind that the bangs might have something to do with the power going out."

"In what way?" asked Penny.

Tamara took a deep breath. "Oh, I don't know. I haven't really thought about it, I'm afraid. I couldn't have guessed..."

Her words faded away. She looked at Penny with an expression of despair on her face.

"It's all right," Penny reassured her, "you're being a great help to me. And your testimony will be very valuable to the police officers. How much time do you estimate passed—between the end of Max Donner's rampage and those three bangs?"

"Ten minutes at the most, I'd say. Maybe only five?"

"More like five or more like ten?" Penny probed.

Tamara made an embarrassed face. "I'm sorry, but I really don't know anymore. As I said, I couldn't have guessed that something so—how shall I put it?—something so significant had taken place."

"No problem," Penny said. "It doesn't matter."

In truth, an exact timeline would have been very helpful. But one thing was certain: Max Donner's murderer must have acted very quickly. He'd only had a few minutes at the most to perform his bloody deed.

Was this possibly an indication that this man—or woman—was a professional, at least when it came to murder?

Penny turned back to Tamara and continued questioning her. "Could you hear anything else in the hallway just before the bangs, or even after, perhaps? Footsteps, for example?"

Even if the murderer had fled through the window—which was by no means certain—he had hardly entered

Max Donner's room that way. He must have taken the stairs to the first floor and walked the short distance along the corridor to his victim's room, thereby taking the not-inconsiderable risk of meeting someone who would remember him later.

"Footsteps?" echoed Tamara. "You mean apart from the wife? I heard her footsteps when she left—but no one else."

She shook her head vigorously, as if she needed to confirm her own statement. "I even looked out the door briefly after Lissy had left, and her ill-tempered husband had calmed down."

"Why is that?" inquired Penny.

Tamara grinned wryly. "I guess I was curious to see if Max would chase after his wife. Or if she would return ... I must admit I'm quite the fan of family drama. I just wanted to know how the argument between them would turn out."

She narrowed her eyes. "Not a good habit, I know."

Penny passed over the self-critical remark. "So you didn't notice anyone in the hallway when you looked out the door again?"

"No."

"Okay, fine. And if someone had just been on the stairs at that time, you probably would have heard them, right?"

"Certainly. The stairs do creak quite a bit. No, everything was quiet. It was only later, after the shots, that I heard a door open. But it wasn't Mr. Donner's, it was on the other side of the corridor. It must have been

Fabia's—Ms. Sievers's. I talked to her earlier for a bit, you know. While you were out in the parking lot."

She put on another guilty look. "Anyway, Fabia's door opened, she ran out into the hallway—and shortly afterwards someone came up the stairs. It must have been you, from what I know now. Fabia exchanged a few words with you. She also said something about shots she had heard. I didn't want to go out into the hallway again at that point; you don't want to come across as one of those old biddies, lying in wait behind the door like curious cats."

Again she fell silent for a moment, only to continue immediately afterwards: "But then I heard the scream and the commotion next door, and I did go out again. The scream, that was Lissy, wasn't it? When she found her husband dead."

Penny nodded but said nothing.

Tamara took that as confirmation. "Yes, that's what I thought. I saw that Mr. Donner's door was open, that Mrs. Bachmair was standing on the threshold, and that—"

She broke off and frowned. "Oh, you were in the room, you must have seen me. I was standing behind Mrs. Bachmair. Then you sent us away."

Penny smiled. "Curious cats," she said, "no matter what age, are worth their weight in gold when you're trying to reconstruct a crime. And the person who came up the stairs—that was me all right. Just before you saw me in the murdered man's room. I had offered to accompany Lissy to her husband because she wanted

78

to get her purse from his room. I guess he frightened her when he was angry."

"I can well imagine," Tamara said, nodding her head in confirmation. "He was completely beside himself; you couldn't miss it. What was he yelling about—just because he didn't like his wife's outfit? That's ridiculous! I really can't stand aggressive guys like that. Although, as I said, he had actually made a nice impression on me before. It's strange how wrong you can be!"

Tamara's eyes suddenly widened, as if she'd had an epiphany. "But if Lissy came up the stairs with you..."

She abruptly fell silent again, seemingly thinking hard about something. At the same time, she fiddled with her rimless glasses, pressing them firmly on her nose.

"Yes?" Penny encouraged her.

"Well, I mean, she couldn't have killed him then, could she? She ran down long before the shots were fired. And she must have been with you after that if you say you met her?"

"Yes, Lissy came back down to the lounge and had a drink. Afterwards we decided to get her purse and then that she would go to bed. Tomorrow she was going to leave the hotel. As we were making our way upstairs, the power went out."

"But ... then she didn't have a chance to shoot him at all? Or did she?" said Tamara, her eyes wide.

"Had you assumed Lissy to be the killer?"

Tamara pushed a strand of dark hair behind her ear and looked intently at Penny. "Yes ... I did. I mean, she's his wife. He'd just treated her like a piece of trash shortly before, and no one else knew him here at the hotel after all. At least, no one admitted it when you asked them earlier."

"Right," Penny said.

Tamara swallowed, then moistened her lips with her tongue—without taking her eyes off Penny even for a moment. The actress seemed to be enjoying the whole drama—as she was probably secretly calling it—very much. A little *too* much for Penny's taste. On the other hand, you couldn't blame an actress for having a special passion for the spectacles of human life.

Tamara continued, "I thought it was obvious that Lissy would want her husband...."

She broke off. "I mean, that she would be the murderer—I did actually assume that. But now I see that she didn't even have a chance to kill him. Whoever did it must have crept into Mr. Donner's room in the short time after the marital quarrel—and then got clean away again. He was damn lucky none of us saw him in the hallway. Could he have taken off through the window?"

"It's possible," Penny replied.

She eyed the actress wordlessly for a moment, then added, "You seem to me to have a keen sense for crime, Ms. Freyer."

"Oh please, do call me Tamara. We're almost the same age, aren't we? As far as crime is concerned, yes, I have to admit that I'm a big fan of crime fiction. And I do perform in plays of that genre myself. I had a role once in one of Ms. Maus' plays—the playwright who's also staying in the hotel. The lead role, to be exact." An unmistakable hint of pride suddenly sparkled in her eyes.

"Oh," Penny replied, "and you didn't know that Ms. Maus was vacationing here at the Bergschlössl, too?"

"No, it was pure coincidence that we met here. We were both very surprised."

When Tamara spoke those last words, there was a hint of uncertainty in her voice. Not the embarrassed undertone she had displayed just before, when she had admitted her curiosity and passion for human drama; it was something else.

Had Tamara just lied to her? Or had Penny only imagined it?

With an actress, one had to assume that she was good at pretending. But Tamara Freyer was apparently not a skilled liar.

Or am I actually reading too much into this woman's little insecurities? Penny asked herself.

After all, Tamara had witnessed a murder a few hours ago. One was allowed to be a little unsettled after such an experience.

12

Penny thanked the actress and accompanied her back to the lounge. There she looked around for the second witness who had heard the fatal shots: Fabia Sievers, the woman in the floral dress. She spotted her amongst the others clustered around the fireplace.

Fabia had changed her clothes in the meantime and was now wearing long pants and a high-necked sweater. She had also put a down jacket around her shoulders.

Meanwhile in the lounge, the ice flowers had also started to grow on the inside of the window panes. The windows of the old building, meticulously restored, were beautiful to look at, but they did not close perfectly. They were barely able to withstand the arctic temperatures of this frigid night.

The fire in the fireplace continued to crackle—presumably the Bachmairs were making sure it didn't go out—but it wasn't able to heat a room as large as the lounge. In the library, directly in front of the fireplace, the temperature had been much cozier.

Penny asked Fabia Sievers for a word in private.

The woman nodded obediently and immediately followed her back into the next room.

Fabia began to speak as soon as she had taken her seat. The words just gushed out of her: "Oh God, it's so terrible. I wanted to relax, to switch off, to get out of the city ... I have a pretty stressful job, you know. I'm a nurse—in Graz. I don't know if I can be of any use to you at all—"

Penny gently raised her hand to calm the woman down. She refrained, however, from reassuring her with hollow words. *It's going to be okay? Everything is going to be all right?*

No.

It would never be all right again for Max Donner. He was lying upstairs in his room ... and soon he would go into the ground in a coffin, forever.

"I just have a few questions for you, Fabia," Penny said instead. "You don't mind me calling you Fabia, do you?"

"Sure. Please do."

"Thank you. I'm interested in what exactly you heard and observed—at the time Max Donner was murdered. What was the first thing you noticed?"

"The shots," Fabia replied, barely audible.

Penny nodded. "Okay. You heard the shots in your room? And you ran out into the hallway because of them?"

Fabia nodded eagerly. "Yes, that's right. You saw me, didn't you?"

Penny recalled the room door that had been standing ajar behind Fabia. "You have the very first room on the right side of the hallway, correct?"

"Yes. No. 101, diagonally across from Mr. Donner."

"And aside from the gunshots, could you hear anything else?"

Fabia seemed to grow smaller, kind of shrinking in on herself. "No, I'm sorry. I was asleep, after all. I like to take a little siesta in the afternoon, especially on vacation. The bang—that is, the gunshots—woke me up. I quickly got dressed and ran out into the hallway, but there was no one there. I waited a moment to see if anyone would show up. I thought that maybe someone else had heard the bang as well ... or that maybe I could determine the cause. Of course, some time passed before I'd even gotten to the hallway. I had to get dressed first, as I said. But shortly afterwards you came up the stairs."

"Could you guess," Penny asked, "how much time passed—from the moment the gunshots woke you to the time I came up the stairs?"

"Hmm. I was a bit sleepy, I'm afraid, and didn't really pay attention to the time. Six or seven minutes, maybe?"

"All right, thank you. Let's move on to Max Donner. You didn't know him, you say?"

"No!"

The answer was unusually vehement. The next moment Fabia pulled back a bit. "I got to know him somewhat here at the hotel, you see. I'm single, and Max caught my eye yesterday when he arrived. He's—he was a very attractive man, don't you think?"

Penny hesitated to answer. When confronted unexpectedly with a corpse, one did not pay attention to the attractive appearance of the victim. Not to mention the fact that a violent death tended to disfigure a person's features.

Nevertheless, she agreed with Fabia. "It's true that I didn't get to see Max Donner when he was alive. But yes, I think he was quite attractive."

Fabia nodded. "That's why I dared to approach him. Nothing ventured, nothing gained, or so they say. I chatted with him a bit yesterday afternoon when I met him in the lobby—and then at dinner I asked if I could join him. Both of us were alone in the hotel, so how could I have known that he wasn't single? He wasn't wearing a wedding ring and he didn't even hint that he was married."

She sighed. "I should have known he wasn't available. Such an attractive man...."

Penny nodded in understanding. "And your evening together—how did that go?"

"Oh, it was nice—really nice. I, for one, really enjoyed it."

"Forgive me for asking," Penny probed further, "but did the evening end with dinner?" She put on an innocent face.

After a few moments Fabia seemed to understand. "What? Yes, it did. But if it had been up to me—"

Her gaze wandered toward the fireplace. She seemed to lose herself in her memories.

But then, abruptly, she raised her head again and looked at Penny. "Why not admit it? I'm not ashamed of it, and it no longer matters anyway. I suggested a nightcap to Max, in my bedroom, but he declined. I guess I wasn't his type. Or maybe he actually was a faithful husband."

She sighed again. "It's too bad about him."

Penny finished the interview. She thanked Fabia and returned with her to the lounge.

There she tried to talk to the other hotel guests again—but they stuck to their statements. No one admitted to have heard or seen anything. No one had known the dead man.

13

As to the cold dinner that Paulina had served due to the power outage, most of the plates were still standing around half-full, if not completely untouched.

A few of the guests were having a drink at this late hour, but their conversation had soon died away. A sepulchral silence settled over the room, together with the nightly cold.

Penny took a listless bite of the cheese sandwich she had just ordered, because she was now feeling hungry after all—and fell to brooding moodily.

The quick success she had hoped for had gone up in smoke. Solving the case before the police detectives arrived was no longer an option. In theory, the saboteur had given her a lot of time, but in practice she was stuck.

She went over in her mind what she had puzzled together so far. It was not very much; she had two statements from witnesses that narrowed down the time of the crime quite a bit, but provided no real clues about the perpetrator.

Not to mention that one or even both of these statements could be false. People sometimes remembered vital info in a frighteningly inaccurate way—and they also lied for all kinds of reasons. They didn't have to have committed a murder to do so.

If the statements of Fabia Sievers and Tamara Freyer were true, the murderer must have literally vanished into thin air after the deed had been done. Or he actually had escaped through the open window.

Why do you resist this possibility so much? Penny asked herself.

Because such a crime left a classical private eye, such as she was, at their wits end?

She depended on investigating a manageable group of suspects. She was good at that. Asking questions, pointing fingers, breaking through people's reserve, sounding out who hated whom and why, or who secretly loved whom, and so on. Those were her methods—and they had always led to success thus far.

She continued to meditate. How did the sabotage in the basement, which had cut off the power supply and thus communication with the outside world, fit into the picture? And what about the blocked exit gate? What was the point of it all?

Who'd had the opportunity for these acts of sabotage? In the basement ... it could have been anyone. Anyone except the murderer, if you looked at it closely. He must have already been in Max Donner's room at the time.

An accomplice?

The word did sound similar to *complication* for a reason. Accomplices complicated things considerably. Alibis were suddenly useless, statements could turn out to be outright lies, and so forth.

Penny put the cheese sandwich back on the plate. She

had barely eaten half of it, but for the life of her she couldn't bring herself to take another bite.

As for the sabotage at the main gate—at the time only one guest had been outside: Martin Knaust.

He could have cut the power supply in the basement and then blocked the gate. But then he couldn't possibly have had time to kill Max Donner.

And why should he have wanted to commit murder? Just because he seemed slightly mentally unstable?

Penny's thoughts ran in circles. In the end, they came back to the unknown man who must have secretly entered the hotel, murdered Max Donner, and then disappeared, all without being seen. He must have brought an accomplice with him to carry out the acts of sabotage, even if they seemed quite pointless. Perhaps the murderer had simply hoped to gain time before being pursued.

End of story.

Damn it all, this was highly unsatisfactory! No matter how Penny turned it around, it definitely appeared that she would not be solving the Max Donner murder case.

But she was not quite ready to give up. *Sleep on it first,* she told herself.

Perhaps a helpful insight would come to her overnight, after all. And if not, she would do her civic duty the next morning and call in the police as quickly as possible. At the very worst she would fight her way down into the valley on foot. After all, the storm could not last forever.

The police officers would then perhaps make faster

progress as a team than she herself had been able to. They could interrogate each of the people present in detail and thus possibly establish a connection to Max Donner, which one of the Bergschlössl guests might have concealed from Penny.

In addition, criminal investigators had the electronic databases and archives of the police at their disposal, and they had far better ways of performing meticulous background checks on each hotel guest. Sometimes solving a murder case was no more complicated than analyzing a suspect's criminal record....

Some of it Penny could have done herself, given enough time, but tonight it was no longer possible. Especially checking people's backgrounds, the complete screening of their private lives, took quite some time. And you couldn't get very far without an Internet connection.

One could hardly hope for fingerprints on the murder weapon. Nowadays even rank beginners were smart enough to wear gloves. Tiny traces left behind on the dead body, however, scrutinized by a professional forensics team, could lead to a breakthrough in the case. But Penny as a private investigator was simply not capable of such analysis. She generally preferred to solve her cases using only her brains, the famous gray matter by which almost every master detective in the history of criminalistics had sworn.

Maybe she really just needed some sleep and would see more clearly in a few hours. She finally made a suggestion to the others to retire to their rooms.

Not all of the guest rooms had their own fireplaces, but it was possible to keep warm under the thick down comforters on the beds. Extra wool blankets were also available in large numbers, Paulina pointed out. Getting some sleep would do them all good.

In a procession, with candles and cell phone lights, they moved up the stairs to the first floor. All the guest rooms were located there. Above that, on the second floor, lay what had been the former servants' quarters, according to the Bachmairs. The couple had converted them into their own private apartment. In addition, there were a few utility rooms, as well as two smaller rooms that the staff used if necessary.

Penny waited in the hallway of the first floor until everyone had retired.

"Lock your doors," she reminded each of the guests again, although it was hardly necessary. Fear was reflected on people's faces. Everyone would make sure they slept as safely as possible, if sleep was to be thought of at all. Many of the guests would certainly spend the next few hours restlessly tossing and turning, haunted by the bloody deed that had occurred in their immediate vicinity.

Penny herself was also tormented by great anxiety. The most urgent question of all would not leave her mind: *is the killer still in the house after all?*

Even if that were the case, Penny tried to reassure herself, he had already done his deadly work. If there was no connection whatsoever between the guests at the Bergschlössl and the murdered man, as everyone claimed, it was unlikely that Max Donner's killer would look for another victim among them.

Unless they were dealing with a maniac who killed indiscriminately, and who had not yet shed enough blood.

The murder of Max Donner, however, did not fit common serial killer patterns. It was not a sex crime, and a gun was an atypical weapon for a serial killer. People who committed murders for the sheer pleasure of killing liked to get their hands dirty, so to speak. In most cases, they killed by strangling, stabbing, or even through bizarre torture rituals.

Moreover, the gun the murderer had brought with him pointed to a premeditated crime. Someone had arrived with it specifically, because there was no flourishing black market for weapons in this area. Although nowadays pistols, rifles and even deadlier weapons could be conveniently ordered on the Internet, and delivered directly via messenger.

Was Penny putting the lives of the hotel guests at risk with her suggestion that they retire to their rooms and get some sleep? Would she have been better off letting people huddle together in the lounge all night?

It was a question to which there was no clear or even simple answer. Locking people who were under stress or even shock, and suffering from lack of sleep, together in a cold room was a strategy that could quickly lead to chaos. In the end, it could possibly have led to further acts of violence.

No, trying to get some sleep in the individual

bedrooms was the better solution—or at least, waiting wrapped in warm blankets and behind closed doors until dawn.

After all the room doors had closed, and the Bachmairs had disappeared up to the second floor, Penny retired to her own room. She locked the door and left the key in the lock, as she had suggested to the others.

As a further precaution, she placed a ballpoint pen on the top edge of the door. If someone were to break in during the night, the writing utensil would fall to the floor and hopefully wake her. She was a light sleeper.

14

Penny was actually woken up late that night, or rather in the early hours of the morning, but not by her self-made door alarm.

It was voices that roused her from her sleep; more precisely, a woman's voice that sounded angry and frightened in equal measure. It came through the wall right behind Penny's bed.

She couldn't quite understand the exact words. "Get out of here ... will scream! ... Show you ... Leave me alone once and for all!"

A man's voice replied something. They were loud, offended words that were about love. The speaker sounded like a frustrated little boy.

Penny was on her feet in an instant. She slipped on her sweater and jeans and ran out into the hallway—where she noticed that the door to her left stood open. Just outside, Penny recognized the strange young fitness instructor, Martin Knaust.

He was the one who had sounded like a sulking schoolboy. Penny could now also see who his words had been directed at, the woman he was having an argument with—Christiane Maus. It was her room that Martin seemed to be trying to get into.

But the author stood wide-legged in the doorway, blocking his way. Her demeanor seemed as resolute as her voice, but Penny read great relief in the woman's eyes when she spied her in the hallway. "Oh, Ms. Küfer, did we wake you?" she called out, "Mr. Knaust was just leaving." She glared angrily at the young man.

He, on the other hand, clearly had something completely different in mind.

Penny stepped beside him and looked at him questioningly. "Tonight is really the wrong time for surprise visits, Mr. Knaust," she said in a deliberately light tone of voice. Sometimes such a playful rebuke was enough—or even more effective than applying harsh words.

Martin Knaust looked confused and annoyed. He clearly still had a lot on his mind that he wanted to tell Ms. Maus, but now that Penny had shown up he seemed visibly disturbed.

He screwed up his face and finally trudged away. He returned to his room, which was at the very end of the corridor, and noisily slammed the door. He didn't seem to care that he might wake up other guests.

Christiane Maus leaned against the door frame and exhaled audibly. Her silvery-purple hair was misplaced from sleeping, and without makeup she looked years older.

"Thank you, Ms. Küfer," she said, "you showed up at just the right moment."

"Come on," Penny replied, "let's go inside, and avoid any more noise in the hallway. And then you'll tell me what just happened, won't you?"

The author nodded, let Penny enter, and locked the

door behind her. She looked relieved. In the bedroom, she grabbed the comforter and wrapped herself in it. She offered Penny the extra wool blanket that lay close to hand at the end of the bed.

Her room was probably one of the most beautiful and largest in the house. It had a bay window that opened onto a small French balcony, and also a fireplace in which a recently restocked fire was blazing. Despite the circumstances, the atmosphere was downright homey.

Christiane Maus dropped into a fauteuil, offering Penny the small sofa that stood on the other side of the fireplace.

"He's a terrible person," she began without mincing words. "Martin Knaust, I mean. He's been stalking me—for months now. He imagines that I'm the great love of his life, which is completely ridiculous. He doesn't know me any more than I know him. And he's a good twenty years younger than me."

She shook her head. "He's not quite in his right mind. And that's putting it mildly."

"He's stalking you?" Penny repeated incredulously. "At home too?"

Christiane nodded. "You could say that. He's always popping up somewhere. He doesn't threaten me, but still, he scares me. He seems deranged. And he constantly wants me to go on a date with him, to become romantically involved. I tell him every time that I'm not interested and that he should leave me alone, but it's no use. But I have no idea how he could have found me here in the Bergschlössl. He must have followed me."

She broke off and seemed to be thinking something over.

"On the other hand, it seems impossible," she continued. "That he's followed me here, I mean. In that case, surely, I would have noticed his car, what with the lonely roads around here. I could have sworn I was alone on the streets the whole time. Besides, I saw Mr. Knaust arrive at the hotel. He showed up in the afternoon, hours after my own check-in. I know his car by now, you see."

She ran both hands through her short-cropped hair. "I don't know what to do anymore, Ms. Küfer. I thought he would lose interest in me at some point if I kept turning him down, but apparently the opposite is the case. He's getting more and more pushy. At first he just wrote to me. First emails, then on Facebook ... where I blocked him right away, of course. Then he started showing up in person. First on foot, later he followed me by car. At first he pretended to be a fan, asked me for autographs and selfies together. That's not unusual so far. I'm quite popular with people; they like my plays. But this man really is a creep!"

"How despicable! He hasn't gotten violent yet, though, you said?"

"No. But he still scares me."

"I can well understand that. Have you called the police yet? You can press charges for stalking these days, you know that, right?"

"No. That is, yes, I already know that. But I haven't gone to the police. To be honest, I didn't expect much from them. I researched stalking once, as a legal offence, for one of my plays. The result was sobering, I have to tell you. Yes, you can file a complaint with the police without any problems these days. Unfortunately, this does not mean that you will be taken seriously. In many cases women are still advised to be happy they have an attentive admirer. Can you imagine that?"

Ms. Maus frowned angrily. "I didn't want to subject myself to that kind of treatment. I preferred to take action myself. I don't go out in public very much anyway, you know. During the day, I always have my secretary accompany me. And in my private house I have a very good security system. In addition, a handyman general worker and my gardener live on the property. Tomas, the handyman, has work experience in the security business. And he has a gun license. So I'd been feeling much safer lately. Martin Knaust has hardly had the opportunity to bother me in the last few weeks. That this maniac has now followed me all the way here on my vacation...."

She took a deep breath. "I really don't know how he found me. It's disturbing."

Penny nodded. "Who knew you were coming here? Surely you must have told someone about your vacation?"

"Well ... sure. I did," came the hesitant reply. "Maria, my secretary, knows about it, of course. And my domestic staff. Aside from the two men I just mentioned, I have a housekeeper working for me."

"No one else?"

"No. And my employees know specifically not to divulge anything. I don't want anyone to know where I'm vacationing. Otherwise I'd never get a chance to switch off."

15

Ms. Maus jumped up abruptly and hurried over to the minibar, concealed in one of the closets. She took out a beer can, tore open the cap and drank in large gulps. Only then did she seem to remember the rules of hospitality. "Would you like something too?" she asked Penny.

"No, thank you."

The author nodded. She prepared to return to her seat, but then stopped abruptly. A sudden thought seemed to haunt her mind. She brought the beer can to her lips again and drank slowly. Only then did she continue on her way.

When she had wrapped herself in her comforter again, she said, "Someone *must have* talked, even though I believed my employees to be absolutely trustworthy until now. After all, my nephew and Tamara have also shown up here at the hotel. Both supposedly by pure chance—but I just don't believe it. They don't even know each other, to my knowledge. So two coincidences independent of each other? Three, if Martin really didn't follow me and didn't know about my stay here. Do you think that's possible?"

"One moment, please. Your *nephew*?"

The mention of Tamara Freyer, the actress, didn't surprise Penny. Tamara herself had mentioned that she'd had roles in plays by Christiane Maus, so it was understandable that the two women would know each other.

However, there had been no talk of a nephew so far.

"Ludwig Lehmann," said the playwright. "The young man who was going to the valley earlier to get help—didn't he mention that he was my nephew?"

"Certainly not to me," Penny said.

But of course she hadn't asked him about it either. When she'd talked to him, Ms. Maus had still been unknown to her. And after that, she had concentrated on Tamara Freyer and Fabia Sievers—the only two who seemed to know anything about Max Donner's murder.

"To return to your question," she said to Ms. Maus after a moment's thought, "no, I can hardly imagine that so many coincidences could happen all at once. How long have Tamara and your nephew been here at the hotel, then?"

The author seemed to ponder for a moment.

"I arrived on Thursday morning," she then said. "Tamara came the same day, in the afternoon, I think. And Ludwig trundled in on Friday. I approached them both about what they were doing here, of course. But both Ludwig and Tamara insisted that they had merely planned a few days' vacation, and that they knew nothing about my presence in the Bergschlössl."

"Have those two—or at least one of them—mentioned any, hmm, specific requests to you?" Penny asked.

Christiane pulled the blanket tighter around her body. "The same thought occurred to me immediately," she said, looking somber. "That they followed me here on vacation because they want something from me."

"So is that the case?"

"Well, Ludwig hasn't asked me for anything, at least not until now. He's been very nice and attentive to me since we met here, maybe a little more than usual."

She broke off, raising her eyes. "I can guess what he wants, though. He's probably just waiting for a good time to ask me. He'd already called a couple of times in the last few weeks back in Vienna and told my secretary that he wanted to meet me. It was very important, he said. But I didn't agree to a meeting. First, I've been very busy lately—I've been behind on the deadline for my new mystery play, you know. Murder doesn't just work on command, I'm sure I don't have to tell you that."

She looked at Penny as if she were talking to a fellow writer. She didn't seem to realize how odd the comment sounded in light of the fact that there was a dead body just a few rooms away. She seemed agitated, unfocused.

"Second, I must confess that I wanted to avoid a meeting with Ludwig," she continued. "Such engagements almost always end with him asking me for money. He is a good man, and I love him dearly, but in business matters I'm afraid he is useless. His ideas are usually very much out of this world. So far he has never been able to pull anything off, and he is already over thirty. He must finally learn to stand on his own two feet. I can't go on helping him out all the time; it's not good for him, you see. He will one day inherit my fortune, which is considerable. He is my only living relative. But if he doesn't learn to handle money responsibly, he'll run through it all within a few years. And then there will be no one left to save him. After that he might possibly end up on the street, or even on the wrong side of the law. He's not so great with right and wrong either, I'm sad to say."

She heaved a deep sigh. "At our last meeting—two or three months ago—I told him that I would not continue to support him. At least, apart from the two thousand euros of basic support that I send him every month."

"And how did he take that?" asked Penny.

Christiane wrinkled her nose. "It got a little ugly. On that occasion he gave me the impression that I was nothing more than a piggy bank to him. And I didn't like that at all, as I'm sure you can imagine."

She leaned back in her fauteuil. "Well, I don't want to bother you with my family problems," she said. "It'll work itself out, I hope."

Penny pondered for a moment. "And Tamara Freyer?" she then asked. "Has she expressed any requests to you since you've met here at the hotel?"

The famous author gave Penny a penetrating look. She straightened her shoulders—suddenly reminding Penny of a younger version of the Queen of England. Confident, regal—a woman who knew who she was and what she had achieved. A little distant, but still friendly and sympathetic.

"Tamara actually approached me about a professional matter," she said, "but you'll have to keep that to yourself, won't you? I don't want any gossip."

"Of course," Penny replied.

Christiane nodded. "It was about a role, in one of my long-running bestsellers. *Die zehn Kavaliere.* The play has been going for eight years at the Volkstheater and is still regularly sold out. Ms. Freyer played the lead role for years—until she was, um, let go, because her performance had become unreliable. Some days she was great, on others she faced massive criticism. I don't usually get involved in such matters at all; I just write the plays. The cast, the staging and all that are taken care of by the respective theater directors. But of course they do value my opinion. If I stand up for an actor, that carries weight. And that's what Ms. Freyer was speculating on. She asked me yesterday if I couldn't give her the role back..."

"And did you promise her that you would stand up for her?"

Christiane pressed her lips together. Brusquely, she shook her head. "No, on the contrary, I'm afraid I was a little rough with her. I didn't like the fact that she'd followed me on vacation with this request—even though she denies any premeditation, of course. But be that as it may, the very fact of asking me to interfere on her behalf, instead of appealing directly to the right person, drove me up the wall. I don't like that kind of favoritism, even though it may be the norm at some theaters. So I turned her down, was perhaps a little too gruff with her. I told her that she lacked talent and that she would never be a really great actress. I don't even know what came over me; I guess she really irritated me." Regret was resonating in her voice.

Penny suspected that behind her imposing facade, the playwright was actually a rather soft-hearted person, which probably meant that she was taken advantage of rather regularly.

"How did Ms. Freyer take your rejection?" Penny continued. "She obviously didn't leave right away."

"She didn't. She did not comment further, nor did she make any attempt to continue the conversation. However, it took place only today—yesterday morning. I have a suspicion that she may want to try again."

Christiane rolled her eyes, but then put on a friendly smile. "Listen, Ms. Küfer, I thank you for your sympathy. For listening to me, and for driving Mr. Knaust away. Shall we go back to sleep? I'm exhausted. This murder ... it was so terrible."

Her voice broke and all at once she looked like she was fighting tears.

Penny rose and gently put a hand on her shoulder. "Get some sleep," she said. "I'll try to do the same."

The storm was still rattling the shutters. It had not abated one bit; on the contrary, it seemed to be raging around the old house with renewed fury and determination. It was as if it didn't want to give up until it had torn the Bergschlössl down.

Penny wished Ms. Maus a good night and returned to her own room.

A murderer and a stalker in the same hotel, what a strange coincidence. What was it all about?

The fact that these three people had followed the famous author here at the same time could not simply be a twist of fate. Martin Knaust, who saw in Christiane the love of his life and stalked her persistently, Ludwig Lehmann, who was probably after his aunt's money, and finally Tamara Freyer, who wanted to gain a career advantage. There had to be something more than mere coincidence behind this meeting, here in the solitude of the mountains.

But all this probably had nothing to do with the murder of Max Donner. Or did it?

How could these events be related?

None of the people in question had known the murdered lawyer, at least according to their own statements. As an investigator, one had to dig a little deeper—but the police would take care of that.

Penny resigned herself to the fact that she wasn't going to get anywhere on this tonight, as much as she disliked to admit it. She threw a few more logs on the fire in her room, which had burned almost all the way down, then she crawled under the covers. She was dog-tired and cold.

But no sooner had she fallen asleep than someone screamed again.

16

Penny started up. Had she only dreamed the screaming?

She listened into the darkness while her heart was
drumming wildly in her chest. The storm was still
howling around the house, but there was nothing else.

No, wait. That wasn't the storm. That howl had
sounded different, somehow ... human? Yes, that was
it.

She searched for the bedside lamp switch with her
hand outstretched—until she remembered that there
was no electricity. She listened again. Was someone
crying? Were there voices murmuring in the background? Or had strange dreams haunted her all the
way into her waking hours?

She fumbled in the darkness for her cell phone, which
she had placed on the nightstand, found it and tapped
the display. It came to life.

She read off the time: 3:35 a.m. She must have slept a
few hours after all. It didn't change the fact that she felt
completely drained.

Again, she heard the howling. It was a crying, a sobbing—and it was coming through the wall of the neighboring room. Was Christiane Maus in trouble again?
Or was she just being haunted by violent nightmares?

Penny rubbed her eyes, lying there indecisively for a

moment. Yes, there were voices too. Definitely; excited, frightened voices. Or was it just one? The voice of a man?

She gave herself a wakening jolt, straightened up and jumped out of bed. Quickly she gathered some clothes and slipped into them. She paid no attention to what she put on; it had to be fast. Not a minute later, she was rushing out into the hallway.

The door of the neighboring room, which Christiane Maus occupied, was ajar. Penny pushed it open carefully—and bounced backward.

In the anteroom, the author lay stretched out on her stomach. A large, profusely bleeding stab wound gaped slightly to the left of the nape of her neck. The knife that had undoubtedly been responsible for it lay on the floor, directly next to Christiane's body. A pool of blood had already formed around the playwright's head and shoulders.

But Christiane Maus was not alone.

Martin Knaust was kneeling right next to her, touching the lifeless body, almost stroking it, and howling and sobbing. It was his wailing that had roused Penny from her sleep—she realized that all at once. And he, too, was the one talking incessantly. It was a strange, repetitive monologue.

"Christiane," he called over and over again, "please come to yourself! I am with you. Everything will be all right."

Suddenly, he gave an even more agonized sob and wrapped his arms around the author's lifeless body. He lifted her up, pressed her to his chest, and wept into her hair. He didn't even seem to notice that he was getting blood all over himself.

It took Penny a few seconds to break free from her momentary paralysis. The sight that presented itself to her was too horrific, too incredible.

However, when she was again the master of her senses, she addressed Martin Knaust briskly: "Let her go. Right now!"

He didn't react, didn't seem to hear her at all. She had to grab him by the arm and pull him away from the lifeless author with all her might, before he looked at her in amazement.

At that moment, Simon Bachmair appeared in the doorway behind them, and Penny noticed that his wife Paulina was with him. She pushed into the room close behind her husband—and stared over his shoulder, her eyes wide with terror.

Penny gave the hotel owner a silent look, which he interpreted correctly. He courageously grabbed Martin Knaust's arm and helped Penny keep him away from the motionless figure on the floor.

The young man let it happen. His gaze, however, still clung to Christiane Maus.

"My beloved," he whispered, over and over again. Thick tears were streaming down his face, but he did not put up a fight.

Outside in the hallway, the noise grew louder. Penny heard doors slamming, voices inquiring what was going on, footsteps rapidly approaching. It felt like déjà vu, a repetition of the evening hours—when she had discovered another murder victim in a different room in that hallway. Max Donner.

"Close the door, please," she addressed Paulina with some presence of mind, "and don't let anyone in!"

The hotel owner nodded dazedly, but did as she was told. She was moving as slowly as a sleepwalker would.

"Is she ... dead?" asked Simon Bachmair. He pointed his index finger at the lifeless figure of the famous author.

Penny knelt down next to the pool of blood, careful not to destroy any traces.

Christiane's head was resting on its side. Penny could look into her eyes, which were half open. No sign of life was visible in them anymore—only an expression of the greatest astonishment seemed to be reflected in the extinguished pupils.

Penny carefully felt for a pulse, bent over her nose and mouth—but all to no avail.

She rose and looked at Martin Knaust and the Bachmairs. "She's dead."

The words hesitated to pass her lips. Only a few hours ago, she had been sitting in this woman's room, talking to her. When she had left Christiane Maus, she had been well.

What had happened?

Martin abruptly tore himself away from Simon, who was still holding onto him. When he was free, however, he seemed to have trouble standing on his own. He staggered to the side and banged hard against the wall.

But he didn't even seem to notice the resulting pain.

"Who did this?" he yelled—clenching his fists.

Simon and Paulina backed away, startled. Simon's gaze sought Penny's, and the accusation that lay in his eyes was plain to see. *He did it, didn't he? Martin Knaust is the murderer.*

That was what it looked like. After all, Penny had found the young man half-bent over Christiane's body.

17

Before Penny could pursue the thought any further, Martin Knaust was moving again.

"I will avenge your death, my beloved!" he cried. "Whoever did this to you will pay for it, I swear it on my life!"

His face reflected an expression of holy anger, and his words had the ring of a Shakespearean character's. Apparently, Martin Knaust had not only been stalking a famous playwright, but also living in a dramatic stage world that he had created for himself.

He bent down—but Penny reacted in a flash. She had more of an inkling of what he was up to than actually registering it.

He wanted the knife that was lying on the floor; there was no doubt it was the murder weapon. Martin went down on his knees to reach for it.

But Penny beat him to it. She grabbed his arm in time and could stop him.

"Don't touch," she said with as much authority as she could muster.

She fervently hoped that Martin would be impressed. Psychologically unstable people often responded well to direct, harsh commands.

Sometimes, however, they did not; then they could become defiant or even aggressive. She had to take her chances, even though she knew that Martin was far superior to her in terms of physical strength.

She felt his arm muscles tighten under her grip.

"If we want to find Christiane's killer, we must not destroy any evidence!" she said quickly—again in a firm tone.

"*I* will find the murderer!" cried Martin. "And avenge Christiane's death!"

"It's important that you help," Penny replied. "But not with that knife. Okay?"

Simon Bachmair seemed to rediscover his courage at that moment. The aging hippie grabbed Martin roughly by the arm from behind and pulled him away from Penny. "Why don't you cut out that hypocrisy, man!" he snapped at him as he did so. "It was you, wasn't it? You killed that woman. Admit it!"

A change took place in Martin's face. The holy avenger transformed into a frightened little boy within seconds.

"Me?" he cried—as if he had been accused of stealing candy. "I would never do such a thing. I loved her, after all! When I came here, she was already lying there, all still and, and ... dead. "

He escaped Simon's grip and put his hands in front of his face. Then he sank to his knees, sobbing, and finally to the floor, where he remained crouched as a curled-up, whimpering bundle.

Penny walked the few steps into the bedroom and looked around. The windows were closed, the bed looking as if Christiane had been sleeping in it only a short while ago. Nothing in the room indicated a struggle or an assault. To all appearances, the author had been attacked in the place where she now lay, in the anteroom.

Penny returned there, gently pushed the Bachmairs aside, got down on her knees and inspected the door lock.

The key was inside.

Penny opened the door a crack and looked at the lock from the outside. She couldn't see any traces that indicated a break-in. Not even the tiniest scratch.

She briefly let her gaze roam the hallway. A few meters away, the other hotel guests had gathered and were huddling close together. They eyed Penny in the light of smartphones and candles, only to bombard her with questions in the next moment.

"What happened? Where is Ms. Maus?"

"I'm afraid I'm going to have to ask you to gather in the lounge again," Penny replied. "Go down together— and stay with each other. No one is to move away, okay? I'll be right with you."

With these words she returned to Christiane Maus's room and closed the door behind her.

She could not avoid feeling fierce self-reproach gnawing at her. We should all have spent the night together in the lounge instead of retreating to the guest rooms. Then Christiane Maus would still be alive.

It would have been uncomfortable and cold in the lounge, and Penny would probably have drawn strong protests for the suggestion. People had been frightened after Max Donner's murder, but no one had seriously thought their own lives to be in danger, not even Christiane Maus. To all appearances, she had opened the door to her murderer herself. She had let him in, and then turned her back to him—or to her. No doubt to go into the bedroom. It had cost her her life.

The killer must have struck from behind with the knife, ramming it into the nape of his victim's neck. The wound had certainly not been inflicted from the front.

Penny squinted down at the dead woman again to make sure. Yes, no doubt about it. That's how it must have happened.

By suggesting that they go to bed and spend the night in the guest rooms, she had given Max Donner's murderer the opportunity to commit another act of bloodshed.

At least she could be sure of one thing now—albeit at a terrible price: the killer had not fled. He was here in the house, in their very midst—which changed everything.

Stop, not so fast, Penny admonished herself.

Sometimes her agitation got the better of her and she jumped to conclusions. That could not be allowed to happen.

Two murders in the same place, within a few hours. That pointed pretty clearly to a common perpetrator. Nevertheless, it was not necessarily true!

A copycat could have seized the opportunity—the chance to pin his crime on someone else.

This hypothesis, however, assumed that there were *two* people in the small group of guests at the Bergschlössl who were capable of murder in the first place. What was the chance of that?

Or had the first perpetrator been a professional who had long since disappeared, and only Christiane Maus's murderer would now be found among those present?

When Penny lifted her eyes, she noticed that the Bachmairs were staring at her expectantly. Yes, even Martin Knaust had meanwhile pulled himself up again, standing upright and pressing himself against the wall. His gaze rested on the motionless figure of Christiane Maus.

"I assume you locked all the exterior doors of the hotel and bolted the windows before we went to sleep?" she asked Paulina.

The hotel hostess wrinkled her nose. "But of course. We always do. And even more so during a storm like this!"

Penny nodded. "We need to make sure no one has entered the house," she said, although she didn't seriously believe there had been a break-in.

No, the killer had been in the house all along. Well hidden, in the midst of them all.

"Let's go down to the others for now," Penny corrected herself. "There's nothing more we can do here. If it's all right with you, I'll keep the key with me."

She glanced at Paulina, who nodded absently.

Then they started moving, one behind the other. The Bachmairs led the way, followed by Martin Knaust, and

Penny brought up the rear. In the light of Simon's cell phone, they shuffled down the stairs. Dark shadows seemed to follow them, and the howling of the storm sounded like the dirge of a choir of the dead.

When they reached the foot of the stairs, Paulina stopped. She told her husband to go on, and he did as he was told. Martin Knaust trotted to Simon's side, and the two men reached the door to the lounge within a few steps.

When it had closed behind them, Paulina turned to address Penny: "It was him, wasn't it? Martin Knaust, I mean. He's not quite in his right mind, you can't have failed to notice that, can you? He killed Ms. Maus. And probably Mr. Donner, too. He came in from outside just after the exit gate was blocked. He must have done it."

Penny didn't reply—but that didn't slow Paulina down in her sudden eagerness.

"Shouldn't we try to ... I don't know, take him out somehow?" the hotelier continued, waving her arms dramatically. "We should tie him up and guard him, or lock him up somewhere. We have several storage rooms in the basement that—"

Now Penny could no longer remain silent. She shook her head, interrupting Paulina's flow of words. "I'm not nearly so sure of his guilt," she said. "Besides, he's unarmed at the moment, as far as I can see, and in no aggressive state. But if we attack him, or even try to incapacitate him, his reaction would be unpredictable. Do you understand? And several of us would have to act in a well-coordinated manner to be a physical match for him. We simply don't have the right people here to pull that off."

Paulina screwed up her face, but then she nodded. "Simon is no hero, I'm afraid," she said, although Penny had made no direct criticism of her spouse.

18

After Penny and Paulina had entered the lounge, the proprietress retreated behind the bar, where Simon had already taken his position.

Leaning against the opposite side of the counter—the one designated for guests—was Violetta Herzbruch, the 'crossword puzzler' as Penny secretly called her.

The old lady was not in a good state. Dark circles had formed around her eyes, and her hands were visibly shaking. "Pour me another schnapps, Simon," she urged the host.

He immediately complied with her request. His hands were also trembling as he poured, Penny noticed.

Penny folded her arms to keep warm. Then she turned to those present, who'd gathered around her without being asked, and gave them a brief account of events. However, she spared them the details of how exactly Christiane Maus had met her death.

"It's gotten even colder outside," Simon Bachmair cut in when she finished. "Minus 27 degrees. I checked earlier."

He shook his head. "I wouldn't have thought something like that to even be possible in Austria. We're not in Siberia, after all!"

It seemed to put him at ease to be able to talk about

the weather situation.

A few of the guests agreed with him. "Terrible. Extraordinary. Thank goodness we at least have the fireplaces!"

"Would anyone like another schnapps?" offered Paulina. She was chalk-white, but with a determined-looking gesture, she fetched several glasses from the shelf. "On the house, of course!" she announced.

Ludwig Lehmann accepted her offer, but preferred a cognac instead of a schnapps. Tamara Freyer ordered a vodka with orange juice.

Penny meanwhile took Simon Bachmair aside. She didn't order a drink; she had to keep a clear head. Instead, she turned to the hotel owner with a request. "Would you please lock the kitchen and keep the key safe," she said.

He looked at her uncomprehendingly.

"The knife Christiane was murdered with," she whispered, so the guests wouldn't hear their conversation. "I assume our murderer must have stolen it from your kitchen."

"Oh..." Simon faltered. "I-I haven't looked at it closely at all, I must confess. You think it was one of ours?"

Penny nodded. "It certainly looked a lot like the ones you put out for dinner. A sharp knife for cutting meat and sausages. Lock down the kitchen, will you? We want to at least make it difficult for the killer to procure any more weapons. Although he might already be sufficiently stocked."

Simon nodded and hurried away toward the kitchen.

Penny turned to Paulina. "Could you get me some paper and writing utensils, please? For each guest, if possible. Surely you have that kind of thing in the office?"

Paulina inclined her head dutifully and immediately started moving.

Barely two minutes had passed before she returned with several small notepads and a handful of pens. Both the pads and the pens were adorned with the Bergschlössl logo.

Penny thanked her, then handed each guest a pad and a pen. "Please take a few minutes and write down everything you have observed within the last few hours. Every little thing, no matter how seemingly insignificant. Write down if you slept and for how long, if you heard or saw something, if you noticed anything that seemed strange and could be related to the murder of Ms. Maus."

Simon Bachmair returned at that moment and wanted to re-stock the fireplace with wood. But Penny interrupted him. "Would you be so kind, please?"

She held one of the pads out to him and repeated the instruction she had just given to the guests.

He hesitated. "I wouldn't know what to write down. I was fast asleep until my wife woke me up," he said. "I'm afraid I can't help you any further."

"No problem," Penny countered. "Write that down for me, please—and then try to think if you noticed something else before you went to bed, over the course of the evening. As I said, any little thing could be crucial."

He made a face, but then grabbed the pad and a pen

and settled down on one of the armchairs next to the fireplace.

Penny turned to Mrs. Bachmair and asked her for her written statement as well.

Both wrote only a few lines each, then Paulina stood up. She announced that she wanted to make a tour of the house, to check doors and windows, as Penny had suggested. Maybe someone had broken in after all?

Penny let her go. She herself walked around the room and watched the guests write down their statements. She was not primarily concerned with the content of these reports—but she left that unsaid.

After everyone had returned the pads and pens, they gathered into smaller groups and wrapped themselves tightly in their jackets and blankets. No one wanted to sit near Martin Knaust.

Penny, however, settled into the fauteuil closest to Martin. The young fitness trainer was leaning back limply on a bench that lined the wall.

"I have a few more questions for you, Mr. Knaust," Penny began—but that was as far as she got.

He immediately straightened up and looked at her from narrowed eyes. "I won't let you frame me. Go away! I'm not talking to you!"

Penny stayed where she was. In a calm tone, she continued, "You want to find Christiane's killer, you said. Bring him to his just punishment. I want that, too. So that's why we should work together."

He eyed her suspiciously, but made no reply. Penny took that as a sign that he was at least curious.

"Tell me what you wanted with Ms. Maus at such a late hour?" she began. She spoke slowly and quietly so that her words sounded as little like an accusation as possible.

Martin pinched his lips together. "...wanted to apologize," he mumbled. "You were there, at my first visit, when Christiane chased me away. I probably got too close to her. I'm inexperienced in matters of love, you know?" he added with a touch of defiance in his voice. "I want to do everything right; I want to be the man Christiane longs for."

He interrupted himself. "That is, I wanted to. Now I'll never..."

His voice died to a whisper. "I will never see her again. We'll never be a couple."

Tears gathered in the corners of his eyes. He sniffled and angrily wiped them away with the back of his hand.

Penny nodded sympathetically—but wasn't ready to just let his assertion stand. "So you went to see her again," she repeated, "Okay. But at three-thirty in the morning? A somewhat unorthodox time for a visit, don't you think?"

He shrugged. "I don't know what time it was. I couldn't get to sleep, not with that ugly argument standing between us and Christiane chasing me away. I just wanted to see her again, tell her I was sorry. I would have promised her to slow down if that's what she wanted. I would have waited for her until she was ready for us to fall in love."

Penny nodded again. The young man, so powerfully

athletic, was now sitting in front of her with a hangdog look on his face. She almost felt sorry for him. "Go on," she said, "you went to Christiane's room ... and then?"

He swallowed. "The door was ajar, which I thought was odd. She would never have left her bedroom door open, after all. She was a cautious person, and quite fearful in general."

All too understandable when you're being harassed by a stalker, Penny thought, but kept it to herself.

"I knocked," Martin continued. "Several times. When she didn't answer, I gently pushed the door open. And there she was. She—"

His voice broke. He closed his eyes for a moment. "Oh, I'll never forget that sight. There was so much blood. Blood everywhere."

"That is, you found her already dead?"

"Yes," he whispered.

"Was she lying in the exact spot where I saw her myself? Or did you change her position in any way before I arrived?"

He shook his head without looking Penny in the eye.

She went on to ask, "How long were you alone in the room before I showed up? Or rather, did you see anyone else before I came? Or did you hear them, perhaps?"

"I don't know. Didn't pay attention to it. But you got there pretty fast, I think. A few minutes at most. And I didn't change anything. I just wanted to wake Christiane up. I thought I could still save her."

He nodded vigorously a few times. "Yes, that's what I

wanted. Save her. Protect her. From all evil, you know?"

"I understand," Penny said, though in truth she would never have been able to comprehend the workings of an obsessive stalker's mind.

He sniffled into the sleeve of his sweater, which he had probably misused as a handkerchief before. The cotton fabric was completely soaked and wrinkled.

At her back, Penny heard the steady groaning and vibrating of the window panes, still being rattled by the storm.

What a night, went through her head. The few hours of sleep had hardly helped her to feel fresher and more rested; quite the opposite. Her body felt heavy, tired and cold, and thoughts seemed to find their way into her brain only with difficulty.

She shook her head briskly, rubbing her temples with the heels of her hands. She needed full possession of her mental powers. She could sleep later!

Taking a deep breath she said, "*You* committed those acts of sabotage, didn't you, Mr. Knaust?"

She was careful not to make her words sound like an accusation—more like a conversation among friends, admitting to one childish act or another.

But the strategy didn't work. Martin immediately went on the defensive. In a dramatic gesture, he raised his eyebrows and pursed his lips. "What? No! That's not true!"

"You were the only one outside at the time when the main gate was blocked," Penny replied in a still emphatically calm tone. "I looked out the window just before, and it was still open then. And right afterwards all the guests of the house gathered in the lounge together with the Bachmairs. So everyone has an alibi for this particular deed, Mr. Knaust. Everyone except you."

He jumped up abruptly. "Leave me alone already!" he hissed.

He looked around the room indecisively for a moment, then hurried away. He headed for another corner of the lounge where no one was sitting and settled there, facing the wall.

Penny did not follow him.

Instead she returned to the bar, where Paulina had just positioned herself again.

The landlady shook her head as Penny approached her. "I'm sure all the doors and windows are locked," she said. "I'm positive no one broke in." A deep crease had formed on her forehead.

Penny knew all too well what that meant: Christiane Maus's killer was no stranger, as she had already suspected.

She asked Paulina for a bottle of Coke. There would be no coffee without hot water, but the sweet fizzy drink also contained a reasonable amount of caffeine. A little push to keep her awake and thinking clearly.

As she was pouring her glass, two people appeared at the same time next to Penny: Ludwig Lehmann and Lissy Donner.

"Can I talk to you for a minute, Ms. Küfer," the two said as if from the same mouth.

Lissy giggled nervously. "Eerie," she whispered, "like

an echo. But I'm happy to let you go first, Ludwig."

She turned away and climbed onto one of the bar stools. Her eyes wandered over the liquor bottles on the shelves, but she didn't call out an order to Paulina.

Penny glanced at Ludwig. "Best we go over to the library," she said. "There we can talk undisturbed. And it's not any colder than here, either."

He nodded, turned on his heel and hurried ahead of her.

19

Ludwig got right to the point as soon as Penny had closed the library door behind them. "That maniac killed my aunt!" he said, staring fixedly at Penny.

She deliberately took her time with the answer. She headed for an armchair near the fireplace, where a lively fire had been rekindled.

"Why don't you sit down," she urged him, gesturing with her hand to the fauteuil opposite her.

"I don't want to sit down," Ludwig returned coldly. "There's a murderer on the loose over there!"

He pointed with his thumb to the door through which they had just come. But then he let himself fall into the soft leather cushions of the armchair. He clearly lacked the guts to stand in Martin Knaust's way himself.

"My aunt was scared of that guy," he said. "He's a god-damn stalker! He was following her, harassing her, and he had been for weeks!"

Penny nodded. "Your aunt told me about it."

Ludwig's eyes snapped open. "And you're still sitting here idly? I thought you were a detective!"

"What do you think I should do, Mr. Lehmann?" Penny asked calmly. "Arrest Mr. Knaust? I'm not an official law enforcement officer, surely you realize that?"

He shrugged and opened his mouth. But then he

faltered. He probably had no idea himself what exactly he thought she should do.

He let his mouth close again and mumbled something unintelligible.

"If I were you, I wouldn't be so sure that Martin Knaust killed your aunt," Penny said in the deliberately calm tone she had already used with the young fitness instructor. "It doesn't fit—and for several reasons. For one thing, he's right-handed, and Christiane was murdered by a left-handed person."

"Sorry, what?" Ludwig interrupted her.

"The stabbing that killed your aunt was done with the left hand," Penny explained. "The blow hit her on the left side, in the nape of the neck. That's consistent with a perpetrator who stood behind her and stabbed with his left hand."

"And how do you know that Knaust is not left-handed—"

He broke off. An expression of comprehension flitted across his face. "Oh, how clever. So that's why you instigated this strange little game! This 'Please write down everything you observed.' Right?"

Penny stifled a smile. "Well, of course people's observations matter," she protested. "And it makes sense to record witness statements as promptly as possible, preferably in writing."

Ludwig made an impatient gesture. "Sure, but that was just a side effect. In truth, you wanted to know which of us would grab the pad and pen with the left hand. And who would use their right or their left hand to get the writing done. That's what it was really all about for you!"

Penny nodded. "Guilty as charged."

"But you can cheat on a test like that, can't you?" objected Ludwig. "The murderer may have recognized your intention and deliberately used his right hand! Just to divert suspicion from himself."

"That might be possible," Penny admitted, "but the profile of a maniac who murders out of passion doesn't align with such rational behavior. If Martin Knaust is really our murderer, he stayed with your aunt after the deed was done, burst into tears, and thus woke half the house. Not exactly rational behavior when you have just committed a murder. Such a killer would then not proceed moments later with so much calculation as to deliberately use the right hand to deceive me."

Ludwig frowned skeptically at first, but shortly afterwards he nodded in agreement. "Okay ... you're probably right. So let's assume that Knaust is indeed not left-handed."

"Let's," Penny said. "He writes with his right hand—just like you do, Mr. Lehmann. It isn't definitive proof of innocence, of course, merely circumstantial. We have to keep an eye on Mr. Knaust—as we all have to keep an eye on each other in general," she added grimly.

Tonight, the killer would not get another chance to take someone's life—Penny vowed to herself on her professional honor!

Ludwig's tone shifted to cynicism. "You hardly have

to keep an eye on *me*. I won't stand for that! You don't seriously think I would kill my own aunt, do you?"

"I'm not thinking anything, Mr. Lehmann," Penny replied. "I'm just trying to gather the facts and not let the killer get away before we can finally get the police involved. That's all."

Getting down into the valley was still out of the question. The storm kept up its rattling of the shutters as if there were no tomorrow. The old building, which had seemed so homey and cozy to Penny when she'd arrived, increasingly felt like the last outpost at the end of the world. The cold seemed to eat through the old walls like an evil demon, and the long shadows between the bookshelves did the rest, stirring up fear and anxiety.

"Who among those present is left-handed, according to your little test?" Ludwig wanted to know.

"Lissy Donner and Tamara Freyer. Although Ms. Freyer reached for the pad and pen with her right hand, she writes with her left."

"Then you think she was trying to pretend?"

"Not necessarily. Some people are ambidextrous—or rather, sometimes they use their right hand, sometimes their left, depending on the activity."

"Murder with the left, write with the right, you mean?" Ludwig shot back in a sarcastic tone.

Penny dropped the subject. Instead, she asked the murdered woman's nephew a direct question: "Tell me, Mr. Lehmann: How did you actually know that your aunt would be spending her vacation here at the

Bergschlössl?"

Abrupt changes of subject were well suited to throwing people off their game; liars and murderers alike.

Ludwig, however, reacted calmly. "I didn't know it. It was pure coincidence that we met here. I found the hotel on the Internet, on one of those booking platforms. I liked the house, the location too, and the price was very reasonable. So—"

"Mr. Lehmann, please," Penny interrupted him. "This is about murder. I need the truth!"

The muscles in his roundish face tightened—giving Ludwig a tougher look. "I say that it *is* the truth!" he protested indignantly. "I'm not going to let you call me a liar!"

Penny looked wordlessly into his face, but he withstood the silent reproach in her gaze.

"I have something else for you," he finally ended the silent duel. "To prove that I'm on your side. That I want to help get my aunt's killer."

He gave a theatrical sigh. "God, I can't believe I have to still prove it! I loved Aunt Christiane like my own mother. And she took care of me like that, too. She was always there for me, you know?"

Penny tilted her head, but didn't take her eyes off him. "Tell me," she urged.

He hunched his shoulders. "It's just a little thing. I don't know if it's important; it probably doesn't mean anything. But here it is: before we went to bed you asked us if anyone had known this Max Donner. And everyone said they didn't."

"Yes...?"

"Well, Aunt Christiane was lying. I don't know why—and as I said, that's probably not why she was murdered. Mark my words, it was that nutcase. That Martin Knaust!"

Penny did not respond to his renewed accusation. "Your aunt knew Max Donner?" she asked instead.

"Yes, at least fleetingly. I didn't know him myself; that is, I knew his name, but I didn't know what he looked like. It was only when you spoke of the murdered man as Max Donner that I put two and two together. My memory for names is excellent, actually."

"Very good. Go on, please," Penny said. She leaned forward in her fauteuil and followed his words attentively.

"Aunt Christiane once mentioned the name Max Donner to me. It was several months ago. She told me that she had an appointment with a lawyer to make her will."

He interrupted himself and gave Penny a penetrating look. "I'm her sole heir, before you ask me."

Interesting, Penny thought, but didn't reply.

Ludwig continued: "Anyway, this lawyer my aunt wanted to see was called Max Donner. And the dead man is—or rather was—also a lawyer, I've heard. It's certainly the same man, don't you think? After all, his name isn't that common."

Penny weighed the information in her head, but wasn't sure how to interpret it. Max Donner had been murdered first, then Christiane Maus. If her murder was about her will—that is, her fortune—why kill her lawyer, too?

There was not a single incidence of such an act among all the criminal cases Penny had studied in the course of her short, but so far very successful, career. She took her education and training very seriously, and spent many hours in her spare time reading relevant books on violent crime. She also regularly visited websites and forums on the Internet devoted to the analysis of well-known criminal cases.

Wealthy testators died violent deaths with some regularity—but Penny had never heard of a capital crime against a lawyer who'd set up a victim's will.

"Did your aunt indicate to you that she'd arranged to meet Mr. Donner here at the hotel?" she turned back to Ludwig. "Perhaps to discuss a change in the will or something similar?"

Ludwig shook his head. "No. After all, Mr. Donner didn't draw up her will."

"Excuse me? You just said...?"

"I told you that my aunt had an *appointment* with him about her will. But then, when she sent me a copy of her last will and testament a few weeks later, there was another lawyer's name on the letterhead. A Dr. Issey."

He frowned. "I didn't think anything more of it. It could be that after the first appointment with Mr. Donner, Aunt Christiane wanted to consult another lawyer after all. Maybe the chemistry wasn't right between them, or he advised something she didn't like. I don't know. Auntie could be quite a stubborn person when something didn't suit her."

Things were getting stranger and stranger. Had Christiane and Max really met by chance here in the hotel? Just as Martin, Tamara and Ludwig had supposedly traveled here without knowing anything about the presence of the famous playwright?

It was clearly too many coincidences at once.

But a lawyer who was following his client? Or even a woman who had not become his client after all? That didn't really make sense either.

Had it been the other way around? Had Christiane Maus gone after that lawyer whom she had *not* trusted with drawing up her will?

Ms. Maus had checked into the Bergschlössl the day before Mr. Donner—but that didn't have to mean anything. But why had she concealed the fact that she had known the lawyer, even if only in passing, after he'd been killed? Out of the simple fear of somehow being associated with his death?

People often lied about a capital crime, even if they were completely innocent.

But why had the two murders been committed? That was the question.

Penny turned again to Ludwig Lehmann, who had leaned back in his armchair and stretched his legs. "So you are the sole heir, you said. Was your aunt very wealthy?"

Ludwig folded his hands at the back of his neck in a casual gesture. "Quite. Why do you ask?"

"Well, money is one of the most popular motives for

murder, I'm sure I don't have to tell you that."

"No. I'm aware of that fact."

"Forgive me for saying this—but the inheritance comes in handy, doesn't it? You can put the money to good use."

Ludwig's jaw muscles tensed again. "Who says so?"

"Your aunt," Penny replied. "Just before she was murdered."

20

Only a few minutes later, Penny was sitting back in the library, opposite Lissy Donner. Ludwig had left without saying a word about his current financial situation. No big surprise there.

Penny had put a few more logs on the fire, then returned to the lounge—where Lissy Donner had already been waiting for her.

Now the two were sitting close to the fire facing each other, and Lissy was nervously kneading her fingers in her lap. The well-heeled woman Penny had met earlier in the evening had turned into a chalky ghost who seemed on the verge of a nervous breakdown. Lissy's hair hung from her head in sad wisps, and her garish makeup had completely melted away. Apparently she hadn't taken it off before going to bed, or she hadn't tried to find sleep in the first place.

Lissy had brought a whiskey glass, which she was now sipping from. When she set it down, she kept it in her hands and clung to it—as she had done with her drinks earlier in the evening. To Penny's relief, however, she seemed to have restrained herself from further alcohol in the meantime. At least, she didn't actually sound drunk.

"I think Ms. Maus knew something," Lissy began abruptly. "That's why she had to die. She hinted at it, but then unfortunately wouldn't tell me more. But what if the murderer heard it? He must have overheard us, and then he—"

Penny leaned over and gently touched Lissy's arm. "Not so fast, please," she said. "You mean Ms. Maus knew something about your husband's murder? Is that what you're getting at?"

Lissy nodded vigorously. "Yes. Yes! She was going to tell me something about it, I'm sure of it. We were all sitting together in the lounge, after ... after Max..."

She swallowed hard. The words would not pass her lips.

Penny nodded at her. "I know what you mean. You don't have to talk about it. Let's just focus on what Ms. Maus told you. That's quite enough."

A grateful smile flitted across Lissy's pale features. "Okay ... but she didn't really share anything with me after all. She just gave me these weird hints. Like she was going to say something, but then changed her mind. Do you understand? I couldn't make sense of it, but now in retrospect I'm sure she must have known something."

Lissy's eyes widened even more. "I blame myself so, Penny. Maybe if I had asked, if I had been more persistent ... she might still be alive now! Then the killer wouldn't have had to silence her, would he?" Her voice broke.

Penny squeezed her hand, pulling the whiskey glass from her fingers as casually as she could. She placed it on one of the round side tables that was just within her reach—as far away from Lissy as possible.

Fortunately, Lissy didn't seem to notice the little maneuver. She was staring gloomily at the floor and began bobbing with the tips of her shoes.

Penny sank into brooding. So this is how the two murders are supposed to be connected?

An intended victim—Max Donner, and collateral damage—Christiane Maus? Just because she had known too much. An annoying witness whom the murderer had disposed of with deadly efficiency?

What could the playwright have meant by her insinuations to Lissy? Had she seen Max Donner's murderer entering or fleeing the room? Had she heard something?

If that were the case, why on earth had Christiane Maus kept this information to herself? She may not have been a professional investigator, but she knew her way around the world of criminology quite well. For what incomprehensible reason had she remained silent, and thus put her life at risk? It should have been clear to her that such behavior was simply stupid.

If witnesses preferred to remain silent, 99 percent of the time there were two possible motives behind it.

First, the witness hoped to blackmail the killer with their knowledge.

But Christiane Maus had certainly not been *that* stupid—Penny was sure of that. Apart from that, hush money was hardly an attractive motive for a woman who was herself very wealthy.

So only the second possibility remained: Christiane

had kept silent because she wanted to protect someone.

But whom? The murderer himself? You'd only do
such a thing if you really loved that person very much.

Could this apply to one of the people present at the
Bergschlössl? To Ludwig Lehmann, perhaps ... the
nephew whom Christiane had supposedly loved like
her own son?

Penny thanked Lissy for her statement and returned
to the lounge with her.

A commotion was going on there. Simon Bachmair
was facing Martin Knaust in front of the bar counter
and apparently trying to push him away. But from
whom or what? And why?

Penny bravely intervened before a scuffle could break
out between the two men. "What's going on?" she addressed Simon.

The hotelier willingly took a step back. He was clearly
not eager for a duel with Martin Knaust—in which he
would inevitably have drawn the short straw.

The young man stood wide-legged, glaring angrily at
Penny when she looked up at him. "This guy is hiding
something, I'm telling you," he snapped—jerking his
head in Simon's direction. "He won't answer any questions for me, and he won't let me go after the other suspects!"

Simon let out a disdainful grunt—but stayed behind
Penny. "Mr. Knaust felt he had to act as an extra detective," he said. "He's been harassing the guests. Badger-
ing them with questions ... and even threats! That's

really going too far!"

"Come on, Martin," Penny said to the young man. She grabbed him spiritedly by the arm and pulled him along, leading him to one of the empty seating areas, as far away from the bar as possible.

Once there, she said in a deliberately conspiratorial whisper, "Listen, Martin. I appreciate your efforts. You want Christiane's killer caught."

He nodded vigorously.

Penny gestured for him to sit down—which he did after a moment's hesitation. She herself remained standing, but didn't have to look too far down at him because of his considerable height.

"I'm a professional sleuth, Martin. You know that, don't you?" she said. "I've hunted down a few murderers in my time, and I promise you I'll get Christiane's killer, too. Okay? You have to trust me. And you can't get in the way of my work. People here are afraid of you, and if you get too close to them, God knows what could happen. We don't have time for that kind of crisis now, do we? Otherwise, Christiane's killer will slip through our fingers in the end."

Martin looked up at her like a sulking boy. He chewed on his lower lip, stared at the others several times—but no one returned his gaze.

"But I want to help," he finally said. "What can I do? There must be something!"

"I don't know yet," Penny said. "First of all, you can help me by just sitting here. You make sure no one leaves the hotel, okay?"

Such a scenario was highly unlikely, but at least it gave Martin something to do. He could feel important, instead of giving in to feelings of powerlessness that might possibly plunge him into a mental crisis. It was really the last thing Penny needed right now.

She forced an encouraging smile, then turned away and joined the other guests at the bar.

"If you don't mind, I'll return to bed," Violetta Herzbruch addressed her. "I'm cold, I'm dead tired, and I'm sure no one wants to kill me."

Penny looked into the old lady's wrinkled face, marked by strain. She could understand her wish, because a warm bed and perhaps some sleep seemed like a heavenly promise to her.

Still, she shook her head. "I'm sorry, but we'll all stay here together in the lounge. We're not going to risk anyone else getting hurt. Try to make yourself as comfortable as possible; we'll probably be stuck here for a few more hours."

Without waiting for an answer, she turned to Paulina, who was standing just behind the counter. "Would you perhaps have a few more blankets for us?"

"Sure. No problem. Upstairs on the second floor, I'm sure we still have—"

"I'm coming with you," Simon intervened. "I won't leave you alone for a moment from now on."

He cast a meaningful glance at Martin Knaust, which the latter fortunately did not catch.

The young man was sulking in his armchair, keeping his head low. It was almost as if he had fallen asleep—

which Penny thought unlikely. On the other hand, his behavior was somewhat ... well, peculiar. Who could say how he would react? The main thing was that he was remaining calm for the time being.

The two Bachmairs hurried away while Penny looked around searchingly. Spotting Tamara Freyer on the sofa in front of the fireplace, she walked over to her. "Could I please talk to you again, Tamara? Over in the library?"

21

Tamara Freyer took a seat opposite Penny, looking exhausted. The actress had put a down jacket around her shoulders, but she still moved her armchair as close as possible to the fireplace.

The library smelled of old paper and leather—a scent Penny cherished. It ensured that she did not feel uncomfortable in the room, despite the cold and shadows that were far too long. Tamara Freyer, however, seemed less than pleased by the atmosphere.

Penny looked at the actress in silence for a moment, then came bluntly to the point: "Tamara, you knew the murdered woman."

She could have said 'Ms. Maus' instead of 'the murdered woman.' That would have been more harmless, more innocuous, but now she was deliberately trying to upset Tamara a little.

The actress made no reply, but immediately sat up straighter in her armchair and looked questioningly at Penny.

"You played the lead role in one of Ms. Maus's most popular plays. That much you've told me."

Tamara nodded hesitantly.

"However, you were sacked—which must have been painful. That's why you followed Frau Maus here to the Bergschlössl. You wanted to persuade her to give you back the role."

"Followed? No! I had no idea she was here. I met her purely by chance. I told you that already!"

Penny remained quiet for a moment, but did not take her eyes off Tamara. Sustained silence could often build up more tension in an interrogation than accusations and loud words. Some people were quickly thrown off balance by this, and Tamara Freyer belonged to this group—at least that's what Penny suspected. The actress appeared outwardly confident, but that was just a facade.

Penny was to be proven right; her strategy worked perfectly.

Tamara was staring at her. First expectantly, but then she seemed to grow more and more nervous. "What is it?" she finally snapped. "What do you want from me?" Her tone sounded annoyed, and her facial expression was clearly unsettled.

"I'm going to make you an offer, Tamara," Penny said in a serious tone of voice. She spoke slowly, emphasizing each word. "You tell me the truth now, and in return I'll put in a good word for you with the police officers afterwards. I am a well-known detective; I have already successfully cooperated with the police in murder cases." That was a little exaggerated, but the end justified the means.

"But I'm telling the truth!" protested Tamara.

"No, you're not. Christiane Maus herself told me that you had already approached her about the role, here in the hotel. Apart from you, Ludwig Lehmann and

Martin Knaust also claim to be staying at the Berg-schlössl purely by chance—and Mr. Donner as well, with whom Ms. Maus had had contact in his capacity as a lawyer. That's clearly too many coincidences for my taste."

Penny paused and returned to looking wordlessly at Tamara. She made sure to stare as accusatorily as possible. She didn't particularly like such games, but sometimes they were necessary; she was now determined to solve this murder case, and before dawn. After the death of Max Donner she had caved in far too quickly—and had thus given the murderer a chance to commit another bloody deed. That would definitely not happen again on her watch!

The actress averted her eyes. She was tougher than Penny had expected. She didn't just buckle and start talking her head off.

But Penny could also be persistent, and patient, when it mattered.

She leaned forward and raised her voice. "Someone told you that Ms. Maus wanted to spend this weekend here at the Bergschlössl. I need to know who that person was. They might be involved in the two murders."

Tamara's eyes widened. Barely noticeably, she shook her head.

"If you tell me who did the talking," Penny continued, "you'll have a point in my favor over Mr. Lehmann and Mr. Knaust, who have also tried to persuade me that they are staying here at the hotel purely by chance. If you help me, then I will tell the police that you made an effort from the beginning to support the investigation, that you were willing to provide important background information. Otherwise ... well, let me just say that it doesn't go down well at all to be caught in an obvious lie when you want to prove your innocence at the same time. Ms. Maus told me that she refused your request, that she didn't want to give you back the role. And I think she made you understand that in fairly painful words—as far as your talent as an actress is concerned. That's a motive, Tamara!"

"But I didn't kill her!"

"Who knows," Penny said. "So now I'm going to ask you again, who told you that Ms. Maus would be here at the hotel?"

At last, Tamara caved in. "It was Maria Plinsky," she said with a deep sigh.

Penny could literally see the tension drain from the actress's body. Tamara slumped her shoulders and leaned back in her armchair, exhaling audibly as she did so.

"Maria Plinsky," Penny repeated. "And who is that?"

"Christiane's secretary."

Penny nodded. Of course, that made sense. The secretary had been one of the few who had known where Ms. Maus was going to spend her vacation.

"Did you bribe Maria to give you this information?" Penny probed further.

"No! What do you take me for? She came out with it completely of her own accord."

Penny gave her a skeptical look.

Tamara raised a hand defensively. "I admit, I did try to get an appointment with Christiane several times, or at least to be put through to her on the phone. Maria always thwarted those attempts. She's a very efficient secretary, almost a clichéd office dragon. But then last week she suddenly called me. 'Ms. Maus will be on vacation in Tyrol this weekend. At the Hotel Bergschlössl zum Wilden Kaiser,' she told me. 'But you haven't heard it from me.'"

"And Maria didn't want any money for this ... little favor?"

"No, she didn't."

"Didn't you ask her why she suddenly came out with this information so readily?"

"Indeed I did. I suspected for a moment that Christiane was trying to play some strange game, set some kind of trap for me. But it was a crazy notion, of course—she had nothing against me personally. She just thought I'm a bad actress, God knows why."

She grimaced as if she were in pain, but immediately continued, "So I immediately dismissed the idea. I didn't believe Christiane to be that vicious. But Maria said something cryptic: 'I know what it's like to be rejected, when someone doesn't want to acknowledge your talent. Or even drags it through the mud.' Those were her exact words, as far as I remember."

"What do you think they might mean?" Penny asked.

"Of course I probed a little further, but that's all she would tell me. I do have a hunch, though. When I still had the lead role in Christiane's play I went to her office from time to time, and I got along quite well with the secretary from the very beginning. On one of these occasions, Maria confided in me that she herself was writing a crime novel. Or rather a play, like one of Christiane's. Her boss was her greatest role model. She also told me that Christiane had promised to forward her manuscript to her agent as soon as it was finished."

"Hmm," said Penny. "And now you believe Christiane might have broken her promise? That she didn't speak to her agent about it after all—maybe because she didn't think the play was good enough?"

Tamara nodded. "Christiane could be really charming, and overall she was a kind-hearted person, too, I think. But as a critic she came across as really brutal sometimes."

She shrugged. "I honestly didn't think any further about why Maria suddenly wanted to help me, and told me about her boss's vacation spot. Of course, something else entirely could be behind her sudden willingness to talk."

"That's all right," Penny said. "I'm sure Maria will tell us when the police start investigating in that direction."

Tamara nodded. She seemed glad that further attention was now going to be on Christiane's secretary. Perhaps she thought herself off the hook, although Penny was by no means so quick to come to that conclusion.

Penny tried to form a mental picture of Maria Plinsky, the offended secretary who wanted to get back at her employer by spoiling her weekend vacation.

It fit quite well. Maria had probably called a few of the

people who had urgently wanted to speak to Christiane recently—and whom the author was in the habit of rejecting.

Martin Knaust, the stalker, had certainly been in first place on the list. He'd pursued Christiane most persistently, and was definitely the most annoying to her. But Ludwig Lehmann, the nephew who was always scrounging for money, was also a good candidate to ruin the weekend. Then there was Tamara, the sacked actress who desperately wanted her role back.

And Max Donner? The lawyer, or almost-lawyer, of Ms. Maus? He must have wanted something from the author, too—something Penny didn't yet know about.

A concern or request for which he had been murdered? That sounded outlandish.

"You will keep your promise, won't you, Penny?" Tamara interrupted her thoughts. "You'll put in a good word for me with the police? If there were even a hint of suspicion to some member of the press that I had anything to do with Christiane's death..."

She pressed her lips together and gave Penny a pleading look. "That really wouldn't be the publicity I need at this point in my career. Surely you understand that?"

Penny nodded slowly, but said nothing. She was still thinking about the possible connection between the two murders.

Max Donner.

Christiane Maus.

But a motive that could explain *both* bloody deeds just wouldn't come to her mind. She had to dig still deeper.

"Penny? Are you even listening to me? I swear I have nothing to do with this whole thing! I've told you everything, now; I give you my word of honor on that. I wanted to get Christiane to cast me again—if not in my old role, then in a new play. She wrote them all the time. But that's all. I didn't threaten her or anything. And if you ask me—"

She hesitated briefly, but then continued with sudden determination: "I'm telling you, this Martin Knaust did it! He is quite obviously deranged! Or Ludwig Lehman. Such a slimeball, always very sweet to Auntie, but in truth he's only after her money. Isn't he Christiane's only living relative, and therefore her main heir? Christiane was rather rich, you know that, don't you? I was once in her private house at a reception after a premiere. It was a real palace, everything just the finest. And Ludwig desperately needs money, I know that!"

Penny's ears perked up. "Oh yeah?" she said calmly, so as not to reveal her curiosity.

Tamara's head bobbed up and down. "Yup! I happened to witness a phone call ... Friday, it must have been, late in the afternoon. It was already dark outside, but not as stormy and cold as it is now. I was returning from a walk when Ludwig was on the phone in the booth next to the reception. He was leaning with his back against the door and didn't notice me. He probably thought he was undisturbed, and was having such a heated discussion on the phone that I could clearly understand his words: 'You can count on me, dude. I'll get the money, and we'll make a fortune with those nags, just like we planned. Just in time for...' Then he mentioned some date. I can't remember what it was. But he's clearly strapped for cash, if you ask me!"

Nags, Penny repeated in her mind. As in horses? Was this about a new business idea? From what Christiane had told her, her nephew was regularly coming up with new business opportunities—but Christiane always thought they were nonsense and rejected them.

"I immediately thought of horse racing when he mentioned 'those nags,'" Tamara interrupted Penny's thoughts. "Betting debts, you know? That kind of thing can get uncomfortable very quickly, especially if you get involved with the wrong people. I had a friend once who was addicted to gambling..."

22

"Surely Ludwig was trying to scrounge money from his aunt, don't you think?" Tamara continued. "She refuses, he kills her and he inherits. Bang!"

What had Christiane Maus said about her nephew when she had still been alive? The words echoed in Penny's ears: *Sometimes I think I'm just a piggy bank for him.*

Had Ludwig become a murderer in order to break open his piggy bank?

Christiane's nephew did not seem like a person who was passionate or aggressive enough to kill without conscience, at least under normal circumstances.

But if he was under great financial pressure, possibly threatened by creditors who were not to be trifled with ... perhaps it would have driven him to the extreme. Or the partner he had spoken to in the phone booth might have incited him to murder his aunt. Could this man on the phone be the accomplice Penny had already been pondering?

In any case, the chances were good that Ludwig Lehmann was in the hotel for precisely that reason: because he urgently needed money. Money that his aunt had—but she had been avoiding him for weeks. He had probably called the secretary several times, wanting to talk to Christiane. And then Maria had suddenly been all too willing to reveal her employer's vacation spot. Yes, that's how it could have happened.

But Max Donner, the lawyer—why had he come to the Bergschlössl? And why had Christiane denied knowing him? She had not done so with any of the other people who had appeared at the hotel seemingly by chance—but in truth with a clear purpose—neither with Martin Knaust, nor with Ludwig, her nephew, nor with Tamara Freyer. So why with Max? Because he had been murdered?

Had the author simply wanted to avoid being dragged into a murder case? Had she, like Tamara, feared bad publicity that could have damaged her reputation?

Penny decided to take another look around the murdered lawyer's room. Maybe she could find some clue there as to what he had been doing at the hotel. Or why someone had decided to kill him.

She had to sift through his personal belongings. He'd had a laptop with him, and certainly a cell phone. She would have to be careful not to destroy any evidence, or better still snoop around so inconspicuously that the police would never even notice it.

She had deliberately left her detective equipment at home, because after all she had been planning to go on vacation, but fortunately there was still a package of rubber gloves and evidence bags in the outside compartment of her suitcase. She would not use the latter; she had no intention of committing a crime by removing anything from the scene. But the gloves would come in handy. The police mustn't end up finding her fingerprints in the dead man's room.

She stood up. "Come, Tamara, we will return to the others in the lounge."

The actress was immediately on her feet. She looked very relieved that her one-on-one with Penny was finally over.

Penny decided to go to her room briefly to retrieve the gloves and then subject Max Donner's room to the search she had planned. Tamara strode toward the bar counter, fixing her gaze on the liquor bottles on the shelf. Presumably she was longing for a drink that would warm her up.

Penny, however, went straight through the lounge and headed for the exit.

"Where are you going in such a hurry, Ms. Küfer?" she heard a man's voice at her back.

She walked straight on, pretending not to have heard anything.

But it was no use. The voice became louder, almost penetrating. "*Ms. Küfer?*"

Penny sighed inwardly. She stopped and turned around.

It was Simon Bachmair who had addressed her. She would not have thought him capable of adopting such a head-teacher tone. Now he was looking at her in a challenging, almost combative way—a strange contrast to the hippie style of his clothes.

The courage of this man seemed to come and go. At certain moments the hotelier appeared quite brisk, only to lapse into timidity again shortly thereafter.

Quite strange, Penny thought.

Maybe she should take a closer look at Simon Bachmair. For the life of her, she couldn't imagine why he of all people would have anything to do with the murders, but she was determined not to ignore any possibility, no matter how far-fetched. Thoroughness sometimes led to success where logic and a detective's instinct let one down. But first she wanted to search Max Donner's room.

"I'm going upstairs," she said tersely, but with what she hoped was authority. "I want to take another look around the first crime scene."

Simon circled the counter and approached her. He seemed hesitant, but at the same time his facial features reflected determination.

"I think you should stay here with us," he said. "Why don't we leave the investigative work to the police, so that everything is in its proper order?"

Why this sudden change of heart? Penny asked herself—but before she could reply, Simon got unexpected help. From Fabia Sievers, the wallflower, of all people. Penny really hadn't expected that.

"Who's to say you're not going to destroy evidence?" the young woman commented.

Her voice sounded squeaky and shy, but Simon gratefully picked up on her words. "Yes, exactly," he agreed. "We only have your word for it that you're really a security consultant. You may even end up being..."

He broke off.

"End up being *what*?" said Penny. "The killer?"

Her irritation grew, even as she concluded at that moment that perhaps Simon's behavior was not so unusual after all.

The people in the Bergschlössl had been under great stress for hours. Two murders had occurred in their midst, and on top of that there was the storm, the cold and the darkness. Not to mention the lack of sleep.

No wonder, really, that all of our distrust is growing, Penny thought.

If even the smallest incident now occurred, people might turn against each other. She could not let that happen; nevertheless, she was not willing to let her investigation be spoiled either.

"You are welcome to accompany me, Mr. Bachmair," she said in a loud voice.

Self-confidence was crucial now, especially when she was standing up to the owner of the house, of all people. "Let's go up together, and you can make sure I'm not doing anything wrong, or removing anything from the scene. I'm just trying to help. It will still be quite a while before we can hope for the police to arrive. We're still stuck here; I'm sure I don't need to remind you of that."

Paulina stepped up next to her husband and grabbed his arm. "I don't want you to leave, Simon," she said, "stay here with me!"

"Someone else, then," Penny replied, growing impatient.

She glanced at the faces of those present, but they all immediately lowered their eyes or turned away.

"No one?" asked Penny. She prepared to continue on her way. "Well, then—"

"Wait! I'll come with you."

It was Tamara Freyer who had spoken. She stood up hesitantly, put her hands in her jacket pockets and approached Penny. "Let's go upstairs together. I think it's good that you're doing something. That you're trying to shed light on this ... matter."

The actress turned her head and addressed Simon Bachmair. "Personally, I trust Ms. Küfer. She's a pro, and she knows what she's doing. You can see that. I'll accompany her and make sure she doesn't do anything wrong."

Penny nodded to her and started moving.

No further discussion, she thought to herself. Nevertheless, she was careful to keep an eye on Tamara over her shoulder. She couldn't turn her back on her too trustingly. For all she knew, the suddenly helpful actress could have two murders on her conscience.

Which, on the other hand, might apply to just about anyone in the hotel. Penny was still completely in the dark regarding the murderer and his motives. And she didn't like it one bit.

23

After retrieving a pair of rubber gloves from her own room, Penny dug the key to Max Donner's suite out of her pocket.

Strictly speaking, she should not have removed the key from the crime scene at all—but it had also been important to secure the room. Hopefully the police officers would have some understanding on that point.

After entering the anteroom, she turned to Tamara: "Would you wait for me here, please? You'll have a good view of me from here and can fulfill your, um, watchdog function—but we'll need to avoid contaminating the crime scene more than absolutely necessary."

Penny didn't usually express herself in such pompous terms, but when it came to exuding authority, that kind of talk proved helpful sometimes.

Tamara hesitated, but then she nodded. She stepped forward to the threshold of the bedroom and stopped. "I'll keep an eye on you," she said with a smug smile.

And I on you, Penny added in her mind. The actress seemed to like the role of overseer. It was probably only due to the fact that Penny had stepped on her toes a bit during her interrogation in the library. Or was there more to it than that?

Penny set to work, careful not to lose sight of her

companion. She began to look around the room again systematically.

Searching a hotel room was no big deal. In private apartments there is usually way more everyday stuff lying around, and cupboards and drawers are sometimes filled to the brim.

Here, however, there was little to discover. In the drawer of the nightstand, Penny found a pack of condoms, and in Max Donner's briefcase on the recliner were several plastic folders containing papers, which Penny leafed through. Case files, as far as she could tell.

The names of the clients meant nothing to her, and from what she could make out their dealings with Max Donner had been routine matters such as those handled by lawyers all over the country day in and day out.

The front compartment of the briefcase contained a paperback edition of a mystery novel by Dorothy Sayers.

Good taste, went through Penny's mind. But if Max Donner had suspected that he himself would fall victim to a murder that weekend, he might have opted for a different kind of reading.

She gave Tamara a look, which the actress returned, then walked past her. From the anteroom, she turned into the bathroom. She left the door open behind her and, glancing over her shoulder, noticed Tamara peering intently at her. Well, no matter, she had nothing to hide.

On the shelf above the sink she found expensive styling products for the modern man: a can of hair wax, some lip balm, and a small bottle of a brand-name cologne. In addition, there was an electric razor and a brush. Truly nothing that could somehow be connected with a capital crime.

Penny returned to the bedroom and picked up Max Donner's laptop. It was an expensive model in a sleekly designed aluminum case. Penny flipped open the computer with her gloved fingertips and turned it on.

Password-protected, of course. You couldn't expect anything less from a lawyer. She tried the names *Max* and *Lissy*, but they were wrong. It would have been too easy.

She looked around the room. Max Donner must have had a cell phone with him, too—nobody left home without one these days. But where was it?

She had to rummage through all the drawers, as well as the pants and jackets that Max Donner had hung in the closet, before she finally realized that the phone she was looking for lay on the bed under the second pillow.

The pillow was crumpled, but it was on the side of the double bed that Max Donner had not used for sleeping. The blanket was still as smooth as only a skilled maid could make it.

Presumably the lawyer had used the second pillow for reading or sleeping, and then put it back later. How his cell phone had found its way beneath it was another question, but an explanation could easily be found for that as well. Presumably he had wanted to keep the phone within reach, and then later mistakenly placed the pillow on top of it. Or had he deliberately wanted to hide it before opening the door to his visitor—and later murderer?

Penny carefully grasped the device with her fingertips and tapped the display. It came to life and immediately began scanning her face.

You have not been recognized, please enter your PIN, it reported after a few seconds.

Penny rejoiced. What a stroke of luck! Facial recognition might be a safe technology among the living—but if you wanted to crack a dead person's cell phone there was nothing better. She stood up, walked the few steps over to Max Donner's corpse, and held the display right in front of his face.

It worked. Facial recognition didn't seem to mind that the phone's rightful owner was no longer alive. The security software unlocked the screen—and Penny set about sifting through the various apps installed on the device.

She checked Max Donner's last calls first, but he had neither made nor received any phone calls in the past two days. That was not surprising. After all, there was no cell phone reception in the Bergschlössl.

In the days before, calls to and from a wide variety of people had been recorded—but Max Donner had not spoken to any of them more than twice.

More time and scrutiny was needed to discern a possible pattern here; it would be best to go through the conversations in the presence of Max Donner's secretary to match the recorded names with business partners and clients, as well as the attorney's correspondence and current cases.

Penny lacked the time and resources for that, but she was pretty sure that this strategy would not bear fruit in any case. Max Donner's killer was to be sought among the people who were staying here in the hotel and whose names Penny knew inside and out by now. The lawyer had not spoken to any of them recently—at least not on his cell phone.

Next, Penny scrolled through Max Donner's email program, but there was only business correspondence, which also looked unremarkable.

She turned to the Messenger chat—nothing.

There were also no text messages. But she finally found exactly what she was looking for in the WhatsApp chat.

Only two conversations were in the list. Max Donner had conducted one of them with 'Lissy'.

Well, there was no need to puzzle over who this dialog partner might be.

Penny opened the conversation and looked through the latest messages. They dated to a while back and revolved around mundane everyday stuff. *Please buy some milk on your way home.* No traces of romance in this conversation.

Penny found something quite different when she opened the second chat log. The dialog partner was listed as 'Püppi'—clearly a term of endearment—and this person seemed to have been the focus of Max Donner's passion.

Not long now, Püppi, then we'll be in each other's arms

again! said the latest message. According to the time stamp, Max Donner had sent it early on Friday morning. That was the day of his check-in at the Bergschlössl.

Had Lissy's husband been having a secret affair?

Penny continued to read, though to do so she scrolled up to the oldest of the messages and began reading there—in the order in which this conversation had actually unfolded.

I miss you, the woman named Püppi had written—on Monday evening this week—and put three pink hearts behind her message.

Be patient, my heart, was Max Donner's reply.

It will work out, right? Our weekend? Püppi asked on Tuesday.

Penny felt like she could read this woman's concern and passion in her words.

Of course, darling! Max Donner had replied. *I promise you! Only three more days, then I'm all yours!*

Our weekend? Only three days left? Penny looked at the time stamp of Max Donner's answer. It, too, was from Tuesday.

Three days later, Max Donner had arrived at the Hotel Bergschlössl. Which had to mean that he had arranged to meet this Püppi—who was clearly not his wife—here. For a secret love weekend, it seemed. Penny held her breath.

But who was Püppi?

The women in the Bergschlössl started to parade in front of her mind's eye. Which of them was Max

Donner's secret lover?

Tamara Freyer, the attractive actress?

Fabia Sievers, the wallflower? She had told Penny that she had approached Max at dinner and would have been happy to have more than just dinner with him. A blatant lie, because she had all along been his mistress?

Christiane Maus, the famous author who was only a few years older than Max Donner?

Or even Violetta Herzbruch, in the end? Was she living up to her name—which meant *heartbreak*—and did the conservative facade of the crossword puzzler ultimately conceal a nefarious adulteress?

The very idea seemed crazy. Violetta was probably a little too old to seduce a man like Max Donner after all. On the other hand, you never knew.

Paulina Bachmair, perhaps? Would she be brazen enough to invite her lover to her own hotel?

Penny could not imagine that either, but love—or in this case passion—sometimes went the strangest ways, didn't it?

Or was Püppi one of the female employees of the Bergschlössl?

Penny quickly scrolled on.

Thursday, early afternoon, Püppi wrote: *The hotel is quite magical, darling!*

Püppi was clearly a guest at the Bergschlössl and had just gotten to know it. She could therefore not be Paulina or someone from the staff.

As far as Penny knew by heart, all four female guests of the hotel had already been in the house on Thursday afternoon. But that could be checked.

Püppi's next message was: *We have to act like strangers as usual, of course, but the nights, Max, they are all ours!*

Max replied with a message of almost twenty lines about what he wanted to do with Püppi during their nights together. The man had had a very fanciful imagination, Penny had to grant him that.

Shortly after, Püppi wrote: *It's freezing cold here, darling, but everything is beautifully snow-covered. Oh, I dream of making love in the forest, right in the snow.*

I'll heat you up, Püppi! had been the answer. *Not that you'd end up freezing your sweet butt off.*

Max never once called his lover by her real name—driving Penny crazy with frustration. Always only Püppi, or darling or my hot little sweetheart, when he got passionate. That was not helpful!

Which of the four female guests at the hotel was Püppi?

Penny continued to read. Three messages remained in the conversation. They were from Thursday night.

Püppi wrote: *Oh damn, Max! My stalker ... he followed me!*

Whereupon Max replied: *Seriously? Damn it! If you want, I'll give him a good beating, then he'll leave you alone once and for all!*

Püppi: *Let's talk tomorrow when you're here, darling. That's all that matters: finally being together again! A whole weekend, just for us. If only we could finally stop playing hide and seek!*

24

My stalker followed me.

That one sentence changed everything. Penny stood there as if turned to stone.

When the end was near, when you were looking death in the eye, you could see your whole life pass by before you. Like a movie, or at least that's what they said. Penny didn't think she was in mortal danger at the moment, but a very similar film was playing out in her mind's eye. Not her whole life, just the events of the last twelve hours. Starting with her arrival at the Bergschlössl.

She had looked at everything upside down, seen events in a completely wrong light and drawn the wrong conclusions from the circumstantial evidence. She had also misinterpreted the timing of events. And all this was not a stupid mistake, but very cleverly planned—by the person who had Max Donner and Christiane Maus on their conscience.

She read again the messages that the two murder victims had exchanged with each other. These two had not been strangers who didn't know each other, but the exact opposite!

The puzzle pieces of the murder mystery that initially hadn't fitted into the picture, no matter how hard Penny tried, now suddenly came together quite easily.

For example, the fact that no one had seen Max Donner's killer coming or going. Or the nagging question of why Christiane Maus had so willingly opened the door to her murderer. There was now a perfectly logical explanation for all of it.

Now there was only one thing left for Penny to do—albeit the most difficult one: she had to confront and expose this dastardly killer, who was hiding among the guests of the Bergschlössl like the proverbial wolf in sheep's clothing. Before they could flee or arm themselves again.

But how to proceed?

She glanced at Tamara Freyer, who was still standing at the threshold of the bedroom, but hardly noticed her. Her thoughts occupied her fully.

But then a sudden commotion arose outside in the hallway. Excited voices could be heard. One of them was particularly loud—and the next moment impatient fists were drumming against the door.

"Ms. Küfer? You have to help me, quickly!"

That the voice belonged to Martin Knaust was unmistakable.

Penny pushed past Tamara, whose eyes were widening in shock, and hurried to the door. She opened it with so much momentum that Martin Knaust almost fell into her arms.

Behind him, she recognized the assembled guests of the hotel—including the two Bachmairs. They were standing on the landing, talking wildly, and now ventured closer.

Penny looked at them questioningly, but didn't get around to asking for an explanation. Martin immediately overwhelmed her with a tremendous torrent of words.

"Oh, thank goodness, Ms. Küfer, there you are!"

He grabbed her by the arm and continued breathlessly, "I solved the case, all by myself! But now I need your help! Before these conspirators lynch me, do you understand? Under your watch, Ms. Küfer, nobody will dare to lay a hand on me. You are the eye of justice. My guardian angel!"

Penny struggled to free herself from the man's grip. But even when she'd succeeded, he pressed up against her like a child seeking protection. It seemed ridiculous, given the fact that he was half a head taller than Penny and almost as wide as the door frame.

He waved his arms wildly, repeatedly pointing at those gathered, accusing them. "They've conspired, all together, you see. Like in *Die sechs Pilger*, my favorite of Christiane's plays!"

Simon Bachmair broke away from the crowd and took a step forward. "He's completely lost his mind, Ms. Küfer," he shouted—pointing his index finger accusingly at Martin in turn.

"He's scaring us," one of the women spoke up, standing at the very back.

Penny recognized Fabia Sievers, who was pressed up against Paulina, intimidated.

The hostess put her arm around her and took the floor in her turn: "He started interrogating us again—

as soon as you left, Ms. Küfer! And then he suddenly threatened us. He claimed we were all murderers!"

She pulled Fabia tighter against her and shook her head furiously. "We really have to do something, Ms. Küfer!" she added with emphasis.

Paulina's gaze quickly traveled over the faces of the guests surrounding her—as if to elicit their approval. "We have to lock him up," she whispered. But her words were loud enough that they did not escape Martin.

He pushed past Penny, into the room Max Donner had occupied. "Don't let them get me, Ms. Küfer! Once they've taken me out, you'll be next. I'm sure of it! We have to stick together!"

Penny slowly turned to face him. She didn't want this man at her back at all. Not that he would end up putting his hands around her neck because he panicked or something like that; Martin was unpredictable. Maybe even dangerous when he felt cornered.

"Just so I understand you correctly, Mr. Knaust," she began, "you think they all committed the two murders together?"

He nodded vigorously. "That's what I just said—like in the play by Christiane. *Die sechs Pilger*. Don't tell me you don't know it!"

Christiane Maus had been a prolific writer. She had written dozens of plays—of which Penny had seen no more than a handful. But she would certainly not start a discussion about this fact with Martin Knaust now.

Instead, she directed another question at him. "And

170

what motive would the, um, conspirators have had to kill those two?"

He hunched his muscular shoulders. "I wouldn't know. You're the detective, I'm sure you can figure it out. But it's obvious they want to make me the scapegoat! Every single one of them wants to pin the murders on me—and that proves their own guilt!"

What screwed-up logic, Penny thought silently, but did not speak her thoughts aloud. Martin Knaust might know every play of his beloved Christiane inside out—but he hadn't learned much from them.

He peered out over Penny's shoulder at the others, who were now slowly approaching.

Simon walked in the lead—apparently he was having another of his courageous phases. Paulina and the guests stayed close behind him, but also seemed very determined to finally do something about the maniac in their midst.

"Don't let them hurt me, Ms. Küfer!" Martin shouted again. His voice was high and shrill. He pressed himself against the wall in the anteroom and raised his hands protectively in front of his boyishly feminine face.

Penny took a deep breath and moved a step forward, blocking the entrance to the room. Now it was important that she did the right thing—and with enough authority that no one would thwart her plan.

She glanced over her shoulder at Martin, then looked Simon Bachmair straight in the eye. "I know you're innocent, Martin," she said aloud.

The words did not miss their effect. Simon stopped

and stared at Penny in confusion. The others did the same.

Penny quickly continued speaking, looking at each of the guests in turn. "Would you leave us alone, please? I'll clear things up with Mr. Knaust, don't worry about it. Just see that all doors and windows of the house remain locked, and that no one leaves the group, please."

Simon Bachmair opened his mouth—no doubt to say something in reply.

But Penny didn't let him get a word in edgewise. She just kept talking: "I won't need more than twenty minutes with Mr. Knaust. Then we'll meet you all in the lounge."

She gestured for Tamara to join the others with a nod of her head, and she thankfully offered no resistance.

The actress pushed past the wall to avoid getting too close to Martin, then darted out the door into the hallway.

Penny didn't wait for any further reaction, but slammed the door firmly shut. However, she stopped right behind it, pressing her ear against the wood and listening.

A hasty whispering began. "What are we supposed to do now? Has Ms. Küfer also lost her mind? Is she in cahoots with that maniac?"

But no one seemed to have the courage to knock on the door and confront them, let alone physically attack them.

After a few minutes, a woman's voice—which sounded like Violetta Herzbruch—said, "Let's go downstairs. At least it's not so cold there. The two of them will follow, won't they?"

The next moment Penny heard footsteps moving away toward the stairs, then silence fell.

"What are you going to do with me?" asked Martin Knaust.

25

When Penny returned to the lounge fifteen minutes later, Martin Knaust marched in behind her with his back and shoulders straightened, carrying his head as high as would any royal bodyguard.

Penny let her eyes wander around the room.

Yes, they had all gathered here again—the guests of the house and the two Bachmairs. By now, everyone was wearing their warmest winter jacket, and most of them had also wrapped themselves in blankets.

The fire had not gone out yet. The wood would certainly last for a while, but in the meantime the walls of the old house had cooled down so much that the fire was hardly able to spread any warmth. And if you looked outside through the window panes, you'd think you were in a polar region. The flakes drifted through the night incessantly, driven by the merciless storm that just wouldn't abate.

Those present received Penny and her companion with equally frosty looks.

"Would you please position yourself here beside the door, Martin," Penny said, gesturing with her head toward the entrance to the lounge through which they had just entered.

Most of the people were crowding around the fireplace. Only Simon Bachmair was still standing behind the bar—seemingly determined to fill his role as hotel host perfectly until the crisis was over.

As Penny headed for the fireplace, they made room for her. That is, it was probably more like getting out of the way, but so be it, she thought.

She stood directly in front of the fire. That way, she at least had a good view of everyone present. And feeling the warmth of the fireplace at her back did her good. It was almost as if a friend were standing behind her, promising her support for the tricky challenge that now lay ahead of her. Would everything work out as she had planned?

She took a deep breath—and began to speak. She knew that she would not be given the time to beat around the bush, but that had never been her style anyway.

So she got straight to the point: "You are mistaken, ladies and gentlemen, if you suspect Martin Knaust to be the murderer," she began.

She read great skepticism in the looks of the guests, but she'd expected as much.

Turning to the side she gazed over at the young fitness trainer, who was standing wide-legged next to the door.

"You, Mr. Knaust," she addressed him, "are also mistaken, however, in assuming that those assembled here have killed Max Donner and Christiane Maus together. A conspiracy of this kind might make for a fantastic play at the theatre, but nothing of the sort took place here."

"Very true," someone muttered.

"At least she got that right!" another grumbled.

Penny was not deterred. Instead, she held up Max Donner's cell phone with her still-gloved right hand.

"Here I found the solution to our murder mystery," she said, then gave a brief summary of the chat that had unfolded between Max Donner and his 'Püppi'.

"*My stalker followed me,*" she quoted. "That one sentence changed everything for me. I knew then that Max Donner's lover was none other than Christiane Maus."

"What?" shouted an angry female voice. "That's not true! Max didn't have a mistress!"

The voice belonged to Lissy Donner. There was a furious glint in her eyes.

Penny acknowledged the interjection with a nod—and continued: "Mr. Lehmann told me that his aunt had consulted Max Donner in his capacity as a lawyer some time ago. Presumably that's how she met him—and fell in love with him at the very first meeting. Or he with her. In any case, the two agreed not to enter into an attorney-client relationship in the first place. Ms. Maus eventually had her will drawn up by another lawyer—and last night denied even knowing Max Donner. The two acted as if they had never met, although in truth they were having a secret love affair. And this, in turn, went perfectly well until something happened that was probably inevitable in the long run: the wife found out about her husband's secret affair."

"What? No, I had no idea!" Lissy protested. "Max ... having an affair with this ... woman? I won't believe it, we had a good marriage! We've been together for twenty-five years! Of course we've had our ups and downs, but Max would never have cheated on me!"

There was no mistaking the pain in Lissy's eyes. The angry glint had given way to the wounded look of an innocent cub.

Penny, however, cautioned herself not to let that affect her. "Maybe your husband was even planning to leave you for Christiane," she continued. "Püppi's chat messages certainly suggest that. But you weren't going to let that happen, were you, Lissy? *Till death do us part,* was your motto."

Lissy's tone became unfriendly. "What nonsense are you talking about? I'm telling you, we loved each other!"

Penny nodded. "I believe *you* loved *him*. Very much so ... or you probably wouldn't have murdered him. An act like that needs a very strong motive."

Dead silence was spreading through the room.

Then Lissy laughed hysterically. With a jerky movement of her head, she looked around at the others. "You don't believe her, do you?" she exclaimed in a shrill voice. "She's completely lost it. She's probably in cahoots with that psycho and needs a scapegoat now! But I won't let her do that to me!"

She pointed accusingly at Martin Knaust—who didn't like it at all. He started stepping nervously from one foot to the other, but said nothing.

Penny could tell by the look on people's faces that they were rattled. She couldn't give them time to start a discussion. She had to speak confidently, and present her evidence.

No sooner said than done. She took a deep breath and continued, again addressing her words directly to Lissy Donner: "You concocted an ingenious plan. You followed your husband here to the hotel. Presumably he hadn't concealed where he was going—he probably only presented the purpose of his trip differently. Perhaps a work weekend, combined with some forest solitude? Or maybe he faked a business trip somewhere else entirely? Well, it doesn't matter. In any case, you knew where he was going—and for what purpose, too. You pretended to surprise him, as would a loving wife, with a sexy role play. Before you went into action here in the hotel, you looked for a witness in the lounge. Coincidentally, your choice fell on me. At that time you had no idea what I do professionally, but even that probably wouldn't have deterred you. Your plan was perfect. And having a private detective as a witness to your little show was as good as anyone else."

Lissy made a point of tapping her forehead and gave a snide laugh. *Quite mad, that woman*, she seemed to be saying.

But Penny registered that the others were now hanging on her every word. She quickly continued, "I imagine the sequence of events as follows: you went up to the first floor, to the guest rooms. There you knocked on the wrong door on purpose. Not Max's, but the door of the neighboring room. You had to make sure that it was occupied. After all, you needed another witness—

178

this time for your little drama with your husband. Just before dinner, with the storm raging outside, your chances of finding hotel guests in their rooms were good. Right at the first door, you were successful. You met Tamara Freyer, who later testified to everything just as you had hoped. After that, you knocked on the right door—and your husband let you in. I'm sure you gave him a good scare by showing up here in his secret love nest, but he probably didn't let on. He allowed you to enter his room—and thus signed his own death warrant. You didn't hesitate for a moment, but grabbed the pistol you had brought with you. Nowadays it's no problem to get a gun on the black market, is it? Purchasing one is hardly more complicated than ordering a pair of shoes on the Internet. And together with the gun, you'd also procured the right silencer for it. You fired the fatal shots at your unfaithful husband, wearing gloves, of course. After the deed was done, you left the gun behind—but you took off the silencer and I suppose threw it out of the window. Just a few meters from the hotel, the slope drops steeply, and it is densely wooded—decidedly inaccessible terrain. The police would have no reason to look for anything there later. The gun was lying next to the victim, after all, and the shots had been so clearly heard that no one would have thought of a silencer."

"Wait a minute," Ludwig Lehmann interjected. "That's a contradiction, isn't it? The silencer, and that the shots could still be heard so loudly."

Penny nodded. "That's true. But look: the shots that

killed Max Donner and the ones Tamara and Fabia heard a little while later—they weren't the same."

"Excuse me?" Ludwig looked confused. The faces of the others reflected similar perplexity.

"Bear with me, please," Penny said. "I'll be happy to explain in more detail. Lissy killed her husband using the silencer immediately after she came into the room. Such shots are not exactly soundless, either, but in a hotel with reasonably solid interior walls they wouldn't be particularly noticeable. If you heard them at all, you could mistake them for anything. They could well be mistaken for some sound from the television. After the murder, Lissy moved on to part two of her ingenious plan: she put her cell phone to work. She had programmed it to play an argument between Max and herself via speakerphone—followed by her husband's supposed outburst of rage after she left the room. And finally, a few minutes later—when Lissy had long since returned to the lounge—her cell phone would play three gunshots, shots that were so loud that everyone in the immediate vicinity would hear them. Lissy hadn't really needed to record Max's voice for the argument and the tantrum. A computer-generated voice that sounded halfway similar was quite sufficient. Through the walls, the witnesses would not notice any difference. After all, they hardly knew Max and didn't know what he would sound like if he yelled."

Penny let her gaze wander briefly around the group—and noted with satisfaction that everyone was listening most intently to her words.

She went on: "So Lissy's cell phone played Max's apparent tantrum and then, say ten minutes later, three shots—this time as loud as can be. You can easily find the right instructions on the Internet as to how to really pump up the volume of a cell phone. Lissy herself had long since disappeared from the room at this point, as I said. She made sure that the witness next door would hear her running away, crying, along the hallway. She sobbed and wailed loudly—and Tamara would later testify that she was long gone at the time of the fatal shooting. Lissy returned to me in the lounge and continued to play her act. She claimed that Max had reacted to her disguise by throwing a tantrum, and that she had left her purse in his room after the argument. Unsuspecting, I offered to go with her to get the bag. If I hadn't done that on my own, Lissy would have had to get me—as inconspicuously as possible—to accompany her. After all, her husband was allegedly violent, so it was understandable that she did not dare to go back to him alone. If I had refused to stand by her, she would probably have turned to one of the hoteliers. Wouldn't you, Lissy?"

Penny sought the murderer's gaze. "It was important to you that your husband's body be found immediately—to establish that you had not been with him at the time of his murder. Had he not been discovered until hours later, the window of opportunity would have been far greater, and witnesses might not have been as specific as to when the shots were fired."

"My goodness, that's a hair-raising story," interjected

Simon Bachmair. "How on earth did you come up with it, Ms. Küfer?"

26

The hotel proprietor had finally given up his position behind the bar and was now standing in the second row behind Violetta Herzbruch.

The old lady had taken a seat in the armchair closest to the fireplace. "Yes," she now seconded Simon's skeptical interjection. "That sounds like something out of a play by Ms. Maus!"

"Call it an irony of fate," Penny said, "or maybe Lissy was even inspired to come up with this particular murder plan by a work of her hated rival. I don't know."

"But how do you know about the audio recording on the cell phone?" Tamara Freyer wanted to know. "You weren't present in that room, after all!"

"On the one hand, it's the only possible explanation," Penny replied. "What puzzled me from the beginning was the apparent invisibility of Max Donner's killer. You and Fabia have narrowed the possible time window of the crime with your testimonies extremely. You could overhear all sorts of things through walls and doors, and you also looked out into the hallway. But none of you saw, or even heard, how the perpetrator appeared or disappeared. So at first I assumed that he must have fled through the window. The only other possible explanation is the one I have just presented to you: That the murder actually took place a little earlier than we were led to believe—and that the killer was not invisible at all, but on the contrary very deliberately attracted the attention of witnesses in order to thus provide themselves with an airtight alibi."

Penny took a deep breath and immediately continued, "And secondly, Lissy was very clever in covering her tracks, but yet not clever enough. I'm referring to the audio file on her cell phone, which included the argument, Max's angry outburst, and finally the three shots. When the two of us discovered the body, Lissy immediately rushed over to the desk where her purse was—which, of course, she had left there on purpose. The next moment she grabbed her cell phone, apparently to alert the police. I paid no further attention because naturally I was focused on the murdered man. I assumed that Lissy had pulled the phone out of her purse, but in reality it was probably not in there but lying right behind it. Otherwise the volume would have been too muffled. But because Lissy blocked my view with her own body, I couldn't see where exactly the phone had been before she reached for it. And while she was pretending to try to call the police, she deleted the telltale files from her device. True, there was little chance the detectives would want to examine her cell phone later, because after all she had an airtight alibi, thanks to the staged sequence of events and witnesses. But you can't be too careful, can you? The audio had to be deleted, just in case."

"And what was not clever enough about it now?" asked Ludwig Lehmann.

"There was just one little thing that puzzled me: namely, that Lissy reached for her cell phone in such a hurry as soon as we discovered the murder. Supposedly she wanted to make a call to the police—but she had to know that there's no cell phone reception up here on the mountain. After all, the Bachmairs advertise it on their website if you want to reserve a room, and Lissy even commented on it to me. During our conversation in the lounge, she told me that Max liked to stay in hotels without cell phone reception so that he could work in peace. Still, I didn't think much of her trying to alert the police anyway, at first. When you've just found your husband murdered, your ability to think logically might simply come to a stop. It wasn't until later that her behavior became one of the little pieces of the puzzle that came together so well, and helped me to solve the case."

Lissy clapped her hands theatrically. "I must say, Penny, you really have a powerful imagination!"

"Let her finish," Fabia Sievers intervened—and earned a bitter look in return.

Penny, however, didn't need to be told twice. "This is where Lissy's original plan ended," she continued as she let her gaze wander through the room. "After all, she had to have expected the police to show up quickly. There was no cell phone reception, but there was a landline in the hotel. She could not have foreseen that it would be sabotaged. She probably planned to kill her husband's hated mistress only at a later date—maybe not for a few weeks, or even months. She would take care not to establish any connection to the first murder; after all, no one knew anything about the secret love affair between the two victims. But then the act of sabotage presented Lissy with an opportunity that she could not pass up—she realized that we would all be locked up here in the hotel the whole night with no chance of outside help."

She turned to Lissy, who wrinkled her nose in disgust. But at least she wasn't laughing anymore.

Penny addressed her directly: "So you murdered the hated rival as well, and had the idea to feed me the story of the witness; that Christiane had to die because she knew or had observed something that might be dangerous to Max Donner's murderer. No one could be allowed to know that Max and Christiane had been lovers—otherwise the conclusion I ultimately drew would have been far too obvious. Jealousy is probably one of the oldest motives of all."

Lissy addressed the others: "Don't listen to her! She wants to deceive you; can't you see that? I'm sure she's behind these evil deeds herself!"

Of course the murderess was in no position to provide details regarding this insane accusation, and so Penny was relieved to find that none of those present were willing to listen to her. All eyes continued to rest on Penny, and Violetta Herzbruch was even nodding encouragingly at her.

"Go ahead!" the old lady said—and Penny was only too happy to comply.

So she went on, again addressing Lissy: "With this

statement—that Ms. Maus was killed because she knew too much about the first murder, you made a serious mistake, Lissy. You could not have foreseen that, however. But do you know that Christiane had a long conversation with me shortly before her death? She was very outspoken, telling me all about the stalker who had been harassing her, and about the people who had followed her here to the hotel, apparently by chance, but in truth with very clear intentions. Strangely enough, she did not hint with a single word that she knew anything about the death of Max Donner, or that she had observed anything that pointed to his murderer. I found that strange. Why should she have made such insinuations to you, Lissy? While she wouldn't tell *me* one word of it, when she knew I wanted to do as much preliminary work on this murder case as possible until the police arrived? It just didn't fit."

"That's right!" someone interjected. It was Paulina, standing just to Penny's right, pressing as close as she could to the fireplace.

Penny continued, still speaking to Lissy: "That was a mistake for which, as I said, you can't be blamed. But nevertheless, it led me onto the right track—and not continuing on the wrong one, where you wanted to lure me with your story about the witness that had to be silenced. In addition, you made another mistake, or perhaps you were unlucky once again. You committed it before you'd even made the plan to kill Ms. Maus. It was about your husband's cell phone. Didn't you think that there might be treacherous messages on it that he'd been exchanging with his mistress? Messages that you should have deleted at all costs, so that your motive for murder remained in the dark—or were you simply unable to find the phone in the short time you had available?"

Lissy Donner had nerves of steel; you had to give her that. Penny had the impression that she could make out a brief flash in her eyes, but otherwise the killer did not reveal what was going on inside her, neither by word nor gesture.

"If you're interested," Penny continued, "I found Max's cell phone under the second pillow on his bed."

Lissy turned her head away, seemingly bored by this revelation.

The rest of the audience, however, was more appreciative.

"Oh, you did a good job!" exclaimed Violetta Herzbruch. From the looks of it, the old lady was firmly on Penny's side by now.

Lissy cleared her throat and began to speak. Her voice sounded unusually firm, as if Penny's accusations couldn't touch her in the slightest: "So I'm supposed to have taken advantage of the sabotage to murder Christiane Maus? I guess you didn't think that through, Ms. Super-smart Detective. Have you forgotten that we were in the lounge together when the lights went out? And that I was also with the others all the time afterwards, when the gate was blocked outside? That clearly shows what kind of nonsense you're spouting here!"

She turned to the others for approval—and Penny noticed that some of the faces that had just looked at her favorably were now filled with doubt.

"You *took advantage* of the sabotage," Penny said in a loud voice. "I didn't claim you were behind it yourself. Because someone else is responsible for that—who has nothing whatsoever to do with the murders."

She glanced to the side in the direction of the door. "Isn't that right, Mr. Knaust?"

A few astonished sounds escaped from those present.

Penny raised her voice: "Mr. Knaust is our saboteur, I already told him that outright a few hours ago. He was the only one outside at the time the gate was blocked. But he felt he had to deny what he had done. Presumably out of the—not entirely unjustified—fear that he would then also be framed for the murders. Am I not right, Mr. Knaust?"

Penny had addressed him about this during the fifteen minutes she had been alone with him, preparing him for the resolution she was now presenting to the others.

At first he had denied it again—loudly and passionately—but finally he had admitted it. In the end, convicting Christiane's murderer had been more important to him than continuing to proclaim his own innocence.

When he began to speak now, his voice sounded rough. "I meant no harm," he exclaimed in the tone of a schoolboy. "After all, I couldn't know there was a murderess in the house!"

189

He gave Lissy a hateful look. Then he started to explain: "You all know this, don't you: when people are locked up together or in grave danger, true lovers tend to find each other. Christiane herself has shown us this in her plays—in five of them taken all together. Even though the respective murder cases were always at the center of her work, often there was also a happy ending for the lovers! It was an expression of her own secret heart's desire, you see. She longed for a man who loved her unconditionally, who would stand by her when danger loomed large. For this reason I came up with the idea of the sabotage—to create exactly that sort of situation for us. So that we could finally come together in love!"

He sniffled, swallowed hard, but then he pulled himself together and continued: "Fear welds us together, and I wanted to show Christiane that I am always there for her. That I'll protect her no matter what. And when I saw that there was no cell phone reception up here, I had to take advantage of it! It was so easy. Where else do you get something like that these days? I just wanted to lock us up together for a night—and finally make Christiane understand that we were meant for each other. At no point was there any real danger to either of us. At least that's what I thought. I couldn't have known..."

His words died away. He first stared somberly at Lissy, then shot Penny a pleading look.

"I guess the protecting thing didn't work out so well," Simon Bachmair said. His tone was cynical, and the look he gave Martin was scathing. The next moment, he shook his head dismissively. For his part, he certainly didn't see the act of sabotage as a peccadillo, or even a romantic gesture.

Penny could only agree with him. On the one hand, Martin Knaust urgently needed psychiatric care—and on the other, he would have to answer for his actions in court. But he was not a murderer.

"The fact that Mr. Knaust is responsible for the acts of sabotage simultaneously proves his innocence as far as the murder of Max Donner is concerned," Penny explained. "At the time Max died, Martin was first in the basement, where he knocked out the power supply, and then outside the house, blocking the driveway gate."

She remained silent for a moment, then continued: "There were many apparent coincidences in this murder case. Any number of people claimed to be here in the hotel, where Ms. Maus was spending her vacation, purely by chance. Martin, Ludwig, Tamara ... and even with regard to Max, I assumed at first that he'd followed Christiane in his professional role as a lawyer. But the only real coincidence was that Martin was carrying out his acts of sabotage at the time of Max Donner's murder, of all times. *One* coincidence—such a thing is quite possible. Even though I have to admit that it threw me off track; indeed, led me on completely the wrong one. I assumed that the murder of Max Donner had to be connected to the sabotage in some way, simply because of the synchronistic timing. That was sloppy logic, but fortunately I realized my mistake in the end."

Simon pointed at Martin Knaust with an accusing gesture. "Just because he didn't murder Max Donner doesn't mean he didn't kill Ms. Maus," he objected. "After all, we found him hunched right over her dead body, have you forgotten that, Ms. Küfer?"

27

Penny shook her head. "I haven't forgotten. But think about it: how would he have gotten into Christiane's room? And would she really have turned her back on him if he had somehow managed to enter, after all?"

Simon frowned, but didn't seem convinced.

"Martin had tried to talk to Christiane once before," Penny said. "A few hours before she died. On that occasion, she received him at the door and certainly had no intention of letting him enter her room. Moreover, she got so loud that I could clearly hear her next door. And then all of a sudden, in the middle of the night, she's supposed to have willingly invited him in?"

"She's right," Violetta interjected—and looked up to challenge Simon. "A woman who isn't completely crazy would never do something like that. And Ms. Maus was certainly not crazy! She wouldn't have let him in voluntarily, and if he had tried to force his way in, she would have screamed, thus alerting us."

Penny nodded and took the floor again: "Lissy Donner, however, had a much better chance of being let in by Christiane. I imagine she came along with some pretext about Max. That she wanted to talk, now that he was dead. That she had known all along about his relationship with Christiane and was now finally seeking clarification. Something like that. Presumably, Lissy got all teary-eyed, as she had already done with me in the lounge, in the frame-up that had cost her husband his life. Christiane let her in, preceded her into the bedroom—and got stabbed in the back by the murderess."

Penny looked at Lissy, and this time she withstood her gaze defiantly.

"You got the knife from the hotel kitchen, didn't you, Lissy? And the risk that you would be seen in the corridor at that hour was very small."

"What nonsense," Lissy snapped. "That's not evidence, just wild speculation!"

Penny nodded. "Oh, yes. The evidence. We mustn't forget about that, of course. You've been unlucky yet again, I'm afraid, even though you came up with such an ingenious plan. The stalker, whose act of sabotage you wanted to use for your own purposes, unfortunately became your undoing. Because, you see, Mr. Knaust truly was obsessed in his love for Christiane Maus. He pursued her at every turn—and here in the hotel he took advantage of an opportunity that had never presented itself to him before. He managed to install a tiny camera in Christiane's room. So he could be close to her, day and night, watch her undress, and so on. You get the idea."

Penny looked over at Martin, who lowered his eyes at her words. But he continued to stand solid as a rock at his post, a silent guard blocking the exit.

"Martin made a full confession to me earlier when you all left us alone," Penny continued. "As I mentioned before, I told him I knew he was the saboteur and grilled him quite a bit. Plus I had discovered the tiny camera earlier, when I took a closer look at Christiane's room. It was immediately clear to me who must have installed it."

"So?" Paulina interjected impatiently.

"So..." Penny paused for dramatic effect, "this very camera can now provide us with evidence against the murderess. We have a wonderful shot of Ms. Maus stepping up to the window in the bedroom as Lissy approaches her from behind and thrusts with the knife. The perfect photo evidence to present to the police. Mr. Knaust will have to answer not only for the sabotage but also for the installation of this camera, but he's willing to do so."

She turned to Lissy. "You're clearly in profile on the video."

"What bullshit, she didn't even die in the bedr—"

Lissy bit her tongue, fell silent abruptly, but it was too late.

Penny nodded at her. "*She didn't die in the bedroom,* that's what you were going to say, wasn't it? And you're absolutely right about that. The only question is, how could you know that? You didn't even see the body, did you?"

Red spots covered Lissy's neck, an unmistakable sign that she was losing her nerve. Her eyes were wide with terror. "S-someone told me," she stammered.

"Oh, yeah?" replied Penny. "Who?"

She looked challengingly at those present. "Any of you, ladies and gentlemen?"

Silence was the only response she received.

It had been a game of hazard, because Penny hadn't been 100 percent sure. She knew that apart from her, only the two Bachmairs had seen Christiane's body in the anteroom. But theoretically the two of them could have gossiped about it with the guests—even if that was unlikely. Throughout the night, almost everyone present had avoided even mentioning the word *corpse*.

The story about the tiny camera was, of course, fictitious. But it had sounded plausible thanks to Martin and his obsessive idea of true love. Penny's little charade had worked out.

"Ms. Maus died in the anteroom, as you very well know," she told Lissy. "She was killed by a left-handed person—you."

Lissy Donner was trapped, and she knew it. Her gaze wandered around the room, flitting over to Martin, who was blocking the door with his massive body. But then she did something Penny hadn't expected—and she was incredibly nimble about it. With amazing agility, she whirled around, ran to the nearest window and tore it open.

The next moment she was kneeling on the windowsill. A gush of ice-cold air rushed into the room—and Lissy jumped headfirst out into the night.

It wasn't a breakneck maneuver, because the window was at ground level, and the snow outside softened Lissy's fall.

Penny saw her getting to her feet, looking around in panic—and then rushing off, out into the frozen landscape, where the storm was still raging.

Penny hesitated for a tiny moment before following the fleeing woman; certain death was waiting out there.

Martin Knaust, however, knew no such scruples. With giant strides he came running towards her, jostled Penny rudely aside—and the next instant he had also disappeared through the window.

Now Penny had no choice. She jumped onto the windowsill, braced herself against the icy wind and took up the chase.

Outside, you could hardly make anything out. The cold bit down with such ferocity that it brought tears to your eyes. Penny's breath seemed to freeze as soon as she let it out.

Half blind, she staggered toward the gate. Would Lissy try to climb over the wall there and reach the road into the valley? Or would she rather bet on an escape through the forest?

The steep slope in front of the hotel—that would have been suicide; but really, death was waiting out here in every direction, wherever you turned. The snow was at least knee-deep, and despite the thick jacket Penny was wearing, she was already freezing to the bone. It felt like she was trying to cross the Arctic dressed in only a T-shirt.

There was no trace of either Lissy or Martin. Had the stalker already caught the murderer? He was an athletic young man, but Lissy had been several meters ahead—and the visibility out here offered her the perfect camouflage.

Still, Penny had to prevent Martin from taking the law into his own hands, which was to be expected if he got a hold of the murderer of his beloved Christiane. Out here there were no witnesses.

He was a severely disturbed young man, but he was not a violent criminal. Penny could not let him ruin his life with an outright murder. Her sympathy for Lissy Donner, on the other hand, was very limited. This woman had killed in cold blood—and twice.

"Martin, let her go!" Penny yelled against the storm. The words burned in her throat as soon as she opened her lips.

She received no answer. But then an idea forced itself into her half-frozen brain. "Martin!" she cried again, "think of the plays Christiane wrote!"

She bravely ignored the pain with which the cold ate into her lungs. "With Christiane, justice is always served in court in the end, isn't it?" she screamed at the top of her lungs.

She knew only a few of the author's plays, but for those, at least, this claim was true. Hopefully, the same applied to all the other plays—which Martin, unlike her, knew inside and out.

"Do you hear me, Martin? Your beloved would not want you to avenge her. She was against vigilante justice! Leave Lissy to the police. I promise you, she won't escape!"

Nothing. No answer. Only the merciless howling of the wind.

But then Martin suddenly appeared in front of her.

He emerged from the darkness like a phantom. His lips were blue, and he was trembling all over.

"She's gone," he cried, "I've lost her. But you're right—about vigilante justice. Christiane would never have approved!"

Penny sighed with relief. Now she could only hope that her promise to Martin would be fulfilled, that Lissy would not escape her just punishment in the end.

But Penny was confident. If Lissy did not freeze to death in the storm, she would be tracked down sooner or later. She was not a professional criminal who knew the ways and means necessary to evade a manhunt. It was far more difficult to hide from the police for any length of time than people commonly assumed. Unless one had made extensive arrangements, had amassed some capital, and had the right allies. Which hopefully did not apply to Lissy Donner.

28

About half an hour before sunrise, the storm subsided. The thermometer still remained at minus 22 degrees, but as there was no wind this was bearable compared to the conditions during the night.

Martin had broken off the key in the lock during his act of sabotage at the gate. Otherwise he would have confessed to his crime, and unlocked the gate after Christiane's murder at the latest. He had affirmed this several times.

So Penny had no choice but to climb over the wall with the help of Simon and Ludwig and set off down the valley on foot. Tamara, who was quite athletic, accompanied her while the two men took it upon themselves to 'supervise' Martin. They promised Penny not to put him through the wringer, and Martin affirmed that he would turn himself in to the police without resistance as soon as the officers arrived. He wouldn't shy away from jail, as he pointed out several times. His life had no meaning anyway, now that his most precious had been taken from him.

The chief inspector, who was interrogating Penny at length late that afternoon, made no secret of his hostility. He thought nothing of 'housewife sleuths,' as he liked to put it. Nor did he think much of female authors like the murdered Christiane Maus, who brought criminal cases to the stage for popular amusement. At least he refrained from further comments, but only because one should not speak ill of the dead, as he emphasized several times. A half-hour monologue followed, which Penny listened to with increasing amusement.

Her conscience didn't bother her, but she did her best to nod ruefully at the appropriate points and agree with the chief inspector. "Yes, of course your team would have solved the murder case without my help!"

She wasn't looking for praise or laurels, and she had no desire whatsoever to get on the wrong side of the police. After all, the Maus case was not to be the last murder mystery she planned to solve as a 'housewife sleuth.' She didn't care for words of appreciation from this less than sympathetic representative of his profession—it was reward enough for her that she had caught the murderer.

"Surely you will be able to track down Mrs. Donner quickly, won't you, Chief Inspector?" she asked him.

"Of course we will. The manhunt is already on! Don't you worry, my lady!"

He eyed her over the rim of his glasses as if she were some exotic insect, and shook his head. "But really, Ms. Küfer, a denouement with everyone assembled in front of the fireplace—just like in Ms. Maus' unspeakable plays? Was that really necessary? And then a psychopath as an ally to convict the murderess? What a suicide mission—that could have backfired horribly!"

Yes, it could have ... she had to grant him that much. But the risk had been worth it, she thought.

Penny smiled quietly to herself. The word *denouement*, which the chief inspector had just used, had no place in modern police jargon. It belonged to the world of old-fashioned detective stories, or plays such as Christiane Maus had written. Literally, it meant 'unknotting' and referred to that resolution of a criminal case in which the detective or sleuth gathered all those involved around them, to present them with the startling solution to the murder mystery. Fireside lounges, libraries, old English 'drawing rooms' were the preferred places for a denouement.

At the Bergschlössl, this kind of resolution had presented itself quite naturally—Penny had not consciously chosen it, or been trying to follow in the footsteps of those master detectives from days long ago, who were her great role models.

The fact that the chief inspector, who supposedly detested the work of private investigators so much, even knew a word like *denouement* revealed more about him than he would have liked. Namely, that in his spare time he probably indulged in reading a classic detective story from time to time—which, of course, he would never have admitted to Penny.

He pushed up his glasses on his nose and cleared his throat. "Well, Mr. Knaust was cooperative when he was arrested, after all. And we'll probably be able to lock him up for a while. In any case, what he did at the Bergschlössl certainly qualifies as stalking in the legal sense.

In addition, there is damage to property and—"

He interrupted himself. "Well, that's none of your business."

He leaned back in his chair and crossed his arms in front of his chest. Then he pursed his lips. "It will probably not amount to a prison sentence for Mr. Knaust, I'm afraid. A year or two of wellness vacation in one of our feel-good facilities for lunatics. A nice little therapy at state expense—as is usual with such scum."

His disgusted expression left no doubt that he would have considered another form of punishment more appropriate, but he knew that the decision was out of his hands.

29

In the early morning hours of the next day, the police manhunt for Lissy Donner was able to report success: The two-time suspected murderer was found frozen to death. Her mortal remains were discovered in a wooded area less than two kilometers from the Bergschlössl Hotel.

Case successfully closed, Penny thought. This afternoon she would look for a new hotel where she could finally start her planned winter vacation. And on the way there, she would get some new reading material at a bookstore. A fantasy epic instead of a crime classic, for a change? A read where people might get massacred by trolls or orcs, but at least didn't die at the hands of a cold-blooded murderer.

Yes, for now that sounded just perfect.

Enjoyed the book?

Please consider leaving a star rating or a short review on Amazon. Thank you!

More from Penny Küfer:

PENNY KÜFER'S CHRISTMAS
Penny Küfer Investigates, Book 7

Christmas with the family? Penny Küfer is quite surprised when she is invited to a fancy celebration with her estranged mother, of all people.

Waldenstein Castle, the party location and home to Penny's latest stepfather, turns out to be a palace right out of a fairy-tale. The assembled guests, however, seem rather eccentric, and what's more, one of them is a ruthless killer. But he hadn't reckoned with Penny....

About the author

Alex Wagner lives with her husband and 'partner in crime' near Vienna, Austria. From her writing chair she has a view of an old ruined castle, which helps her to dream up the most devious murder plots.

Alex writes murder mysteries set in the most beautiful locations in Europe and in popular holiday spots. If you love to read Agatha Christie and other authors from the Golden Age of mystery fiction, you will enjoy her stories.

www.alexwagner.at
www.facebook.com/AlexWagnerMysteryWriter

Made in the USA
Monee, IL
22 September 2022

14413299R00121